HARCOURT BRACE & COMPANY
1919–
1994
SEVENTY-FIVE YEARS

THE
SHARK
CALLERS

ALSO BY ERIC CAMPBELL

The Year of the Leopard Song

The Place of Lions

THE
SHARK
CALLERS

Eric Campbell

HARCOURT BRACE & COMPANY
San Diego   New York   London

First published 1993 by Pan Macmillan Children's Books, London
Copyright © 1994, 1993 by Eric Campbell
First United States edition 1994

Requests for permission to make copies of any part
of the work should be mailed to: Permissions Department,
Harcourt Brace & Company, 6277 Sea Harbor Drive,
Orlando, Florida 32887-6777.

Library of Congress Cataloguing-in-Publication Data
Campbell, Eric (Eric M.)
The Shark Callers/Eric Campbell—1st ed.
p.   cm.
"First published 1993 by Pan Macmillan Children's Books,
London"—T.p. verso.
Summary: Two teenage boys, one on a shark hunt and the other
traveling with his family, face the challenge of their lives when a
volcano erupts, causing a massive tidal wave in the South Seas.
ISBN 0-15-200007-0   ISBN 0-15-200010-0 (pbk.)
[1. Survival—Fiction. 2. Sharks—Fiction 3. Volcanoes—Fiction
4. Oceania—Fiction.] I. Title
PZ7.C15098Sh   1994
[Fic]—dc20   93-44881

The text was set in Minion.

Designed by Linda Lockowitz
Printed in Hong Kong
First edition
A B C D E

For my daughter, Rebecca,
whose childhood was spent in
Papua New Guinea

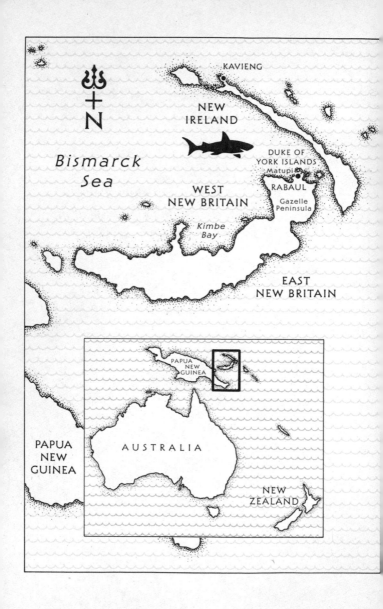

ONE

፨

Today they were moving on.

The town had gone from Yellow Alert to Purple Alert in less than a month. The next one was Red Alert. Evacuate.

They had decided they weren't going to wait around for that.

You couldn't tell anything dramatic was happening by looking at Matupi, the volcano. It hadn't changed in appearance since they had arrived three months ago. It sat quietly at the harbor entrance, its lower slopes covered in dense vegetation, its crater gaping to the sky.

It didn't look dangerous at all.

But that was its cruel deception, and Andy Thompson knew it.

Idling a day away in the town's library shortly after they had arrived in Rabaul, he had come across a report of the last time the volcano had erupted, in 1937.

The report was chilling and had made him look at Matupi with fresh eyes.

It told of warnings that had been ignored; of tremors shuddering through the ground and shaking the houses as though they were built of paper; of rumblings deep in the earth; of great shoals of dead fish washed up on the shores of the bay, their flesh boiled by deep-sea heat.

It told of native people who had been frightened and bewildered. Of village elders, old enough to remember the last time the earth had shaken, who had said that the gods were angry, and who had made the people hold great feasts and *sing-sings* in the villages and kill many pigs to calm the raging mountain.

For days in 1937 the sounds of drums throbbing and voices raised in song had mingled with the shrieks of pigs being slaughtered.

But nothing they had done had helped; nothing had averted their terrible fate.

Late one afternoon the cone had blown itself apart in a series of tremendous explosions, tossing red-hot boulders into the sky and raining hot ash and molten rock down onto the people.

An eerie, terrible night had followed, and the next day a survivor had recorded:

Rabaul found itself bombarded by a violent electrical storm that put the lights out, and this was followed by a rainstorm the likes of which none of us had ever seen. It came as solid water, and the gray, smoky dawn revealed that it had swept away roads and cut gullies a hundred feet deep in the pumice of the hills. I went down to the wharf and saw that its piles were standing in dark yellow pumice that was floating deep around the harbor.

Across the desert of yellow, I saw that Vulcan Island had disappeared. In its place stood a brand-new mountain—a perfect cone fifteen hundred feet high. Steam was issuing from its peak. A mountain had been born.

I was still marveling when my companion, Boko, said, "I think all the Tavuan are dead."

I thought of the great feast and dance that had taken place the previous day. The villages of Keravia and Tavuan were right alongside the eruption. Hundreds who had been there must now be buried under the rock and pumice.

Many times since he had read that account, Andy had thought sadly of those villagers dying in fiery agony in numbers that no one had ever been able to count.

He shuddered now as he sat on the tiny wooden jetty, feet dangling in the warm, gently lapping water. He looked out over the bay and tried to imagine the long-gone island, tried to imagine the water boiling and floating with a heavy scum of yellow pumice.

It defeated even his lively imagination.

Now, apparently, it was going to happen again. The vulcanological station, set high on the hills behind the town, had detected tremors months ago—deep down in the mountain, the liquid earth was seething and bubbling—and they had given the first grim warning that Matupi was awakening again. They had issued the Yellow Alert.

Shortly afterward a ship had arrived and moored at anchor in the shadow of the cone. Several times a day the vulcanologists on board had taken depth readings, dropping high explosives into the water and measuring the time the echo took to bounce back from the ocean bed.

Soon there was no doubt. The seafloor was rising, pushed upward by the terrible, irresistible pressure of the molten lava and swirling gases of Matupi's heart.

At first it was only millimeters a day.

The scientists would shrug dismissively and say, "No worries. It's nothing yet. Just grumbling. It might subside. We'll wait and see."

But it didn't subside; and as the weeks drew on, the pressure built, the seabed rose, and the scientists became more serious.

"That's it now," they said eventually. "It's irreversible. Past the point of no return. It's going to blow." And they ordered the Purple Alert: Prepare for evacuation.

The sleepy town galvanized into life. Someone dragged out the rusty wartime siren, dusted it off, and cranked it into wailing life. Evacuation plans were drawn up, trucks and pickups requisitioned, assembly points organized. Notices appeared everywhere, telling people what to do when the fateful siren sounded. For a time everything was movement as people planned and packed and made ready. With that done, there was nothing left but to wait and watch.

People got on with their lives as best they could, but they didn't have much heart in what they were doing. If their town was going to be destroyed, there wasn't much point in anything.

Anxiety was everywhere. The very air they breathed was filled with the stinging stench of sulfur from the volcano. A hundred times a day people would stop, look fearfully at the gently smoking rim of Matupi, and wonder, *When?*

The nights were the worst time. People had difficulty sleeping. What if it happened at night, and the siren went unheard, and you slept, unknowing, and the ground opened up beneath your house?

Yet people did sleep, fitfully and lightly, bolstered by eternal human optimism.

It won't really happen, they thought.

Well, it wasn't going to happen to the Thompson family, that was for sure, because today they were pulling up anchor and leaving.

The months in Rabaul had been very

happy, but there was no sense in inviting catastrophe. They were used to the perils of the sea, but if you know the sea and know your ship, the dangers are controllable. You can't control a volcano. The only thing you can do about a volcano is not be there when it blows.

So the last few days had been spent getting *Quintana* ready. The food stocks had been replenished, and now the lockers were full of canned and dried foods and the inevitable sack of rice. The sails, which had been ripped in vicious squalls off Bougainville Island months ago, had been skillfully mended by an old Chinese sailmaker and were all stowed ready. The fuel pump on the temperamental diesel engine had been repaired for the thousandth time, so at least Andy's father would not be swearing at the engine for a few days—until it broke again.

And, just that morning, Andy had coaxed the engine to life, taken *Quintana* across the harbor to the main wharf, and had the fuel and water tanks filled to their brims. Then he had brought her back, moored her in deep water out from the jetty, and rowed the dinghy in to wait for the rest of the family, who were in town saying their good-byes and buying fresh bread and fruit and vegetables from the market.

By lunchtime they would be gone.

Andy looked out to where *Quintana,* was anchored. There were about fifty assorted craft lolling, absolutely motionless, on the glassy flatness of the sea.

Whenever he looked at *Quintana,* he was proud. She stood out from the others. Somehow she was more beautiful, more dependable than the slick modern craft. She wasn't young but had a solidity that made her feel indestructible. She had been built in Hong Kong in the 1930s, of glowing, dark teak, copper fastened, and with a huge lead keel that weighed nearly eight tons. Her stern was canoe shaped, and she had a graceful, pronounced sheer that rose gently up her forty-five-foot length. The bowsprit continued the line so that *Quintana* always looked as though she were riding a wave, her bow lifting into it. Even at rest she looked as though she strained to move, as though she sniffed the air in eager anticipation to be off. The top of her mainmast towered fifty feet above her decks and even her mizzenmast, toward the stern, rose to thirty-five feet. When she was fully sailed and in a good blow, she would foam through the water at a breathtaking twelve knots.

But it wasn't her speed or beauty that had endeared her to the family over the years. It was the feeling she gave them of safety. In the worst of storms, when forty-foot waves would send her crashing from high crest to trough, or winds would broach her against towering walls of water, Andy's father would shout, "Don't worry—*Quintana* will look after us."

She always had, and they loved her for it.

In *Quintana* the Thompsons had made their way about the world, seeking everything and seeking nothing, for all the years of Andy's and his sister Sally's lives. Always moving on.

And now they were on the move again, away from this looming danger.

Last night they had studied the charts and decided to head for Kavieng, at the northern tip of the long curve of New Ireland. It was probably two or three days' sail away, though the winds were a bit fickle at the moment, not knowing which way to blow, so it might be more. Anyway, there were some tantalizing little blobs on the map, which called themselves the Duke of York Islands and which might be worth a day or two of exploration.

Andy's eyes moved from the moored yachts and scanned around the perimeter of the harbor. The neat little houses, which crowded right up to the beach, shone whitely in the morning sun. He lifted his eyes from the brightness and rested them on the quiet green of the old extinct volcanoes rising up behind the town. The soft-contoured cones loomed over the roofs like benevolent giants guarding the town. It was hard to imagine that these innocent-looking peaks had been born in such cataclysmic violence. Harder still to believe that it was all going to happen again. He looked across the bay to Matupi, but it was just the same as always. Silent, dusty-peaked, and wisping puffs of smoke and steam against the blue of the sky.

A cheery shout rang out from somewhere behind him. He turned to see his father, mother, and sister staggering down the wharf road, laden with cardboard boxes.

He stood and went to the end of the jetty. The dinghy was bobbing gently in the ripples of a passing canoe, and he hauled on the rope to pull it in. He tied it close, then turned and went back to help carry the last of the provisions.

Time to go.

TWO

ॐ

No one in the New Ireland village of Lorolargun ever called the old man by his name. In fact, most of the villagers didn't know what his name was. Only the very old could remember a time when he was called something else.

Now everyone just called him Old Seabird.

You could see him any day, hunched with age, stumping along the beach, his slender, three-pronged fishing spear in his hand, out to catch his dinner.

When you couldn't see him you would often know he was there from the smell of his tobacco: the heavy, acrid tang of *brus,* the coarse black leaf that he grew himself behind his house and smoked wherever he went.

The young men used to laugh and say he smoked even when he slept.

Sometimes, too, you could hear him. For, as he walked or stood thigh-deep in the lapping waters of the reef, he would sing his songs. His voice was high, age cracked, and faltering.

In the village the old would put their heads to one side, listen, say "Tut tut," and look sad for times gone by.

The village girls, hearing his sad wail, would gather, bright-thronged in their brilliant *lap-lap*s, laugh, point to their temples, roll their eyes, gurgle "Old Sea-bird. Old Crazy," and run, giggling, away from him.

But the girls did not know, would never know, for the *tambu* forbade them to know. Forbade them even to go near his coral-walled enclosure.

His house stood a little way down the beach from the village: close enough for him to see everything that was happening, far enough away for his secrets to be kept from the prying eyes of nosy village women. The Shark Callers' secrets were for men alone.

The house was like himself: old, faded, and leaning a little. He had built it, with love and care, so many years ago that he could not count them now. It seemed, in memory, that all his youth had passed in the building of it.

There he had lived his years, underneath the soft shade of the old beech tree with its tortured, knotted trunk. There, in the quiet darkness, he had worked the magic of the Shark Callers, the magic handed down to him through the generations of his people, and gone out in his canoe when the seas were calm at the time of *lamat*, far, far out to sea, beyond the sight of land, in search of the shark roads.

In time he had learned all the ways of sharks. He had called them and hunted them and killed them until, of all the people on the islands, he was known as the greatest of the Shark Callers, and the rafters and walls of his hut were hung thick with black fins, dried and smoked until they were as hard as wood. But all that was past. The sharks he hunted now were hunted only in his high songs or in the sweet places of memory.

The strong, young men called the sharks now.

The shark was made, so the legends told, in the time of *tulait*, the time when the world pauses to take breath between the end of night and the dawn of the new day. And so, tradition demanded, a Shark Caller must begin his apprenticeship at the time of *tulait*, too.

Now, in the week when the winds had finally ceased their capricious meanderings and settled to a steady southeast blow, the young man Kaleku, the first of the new *lamat*'s Shark Callers, arrived at Old Seabird's house just before dawn.

He stood outside and called gently in the dawn silence to waken the old man.

"*Larangam*," he called. "*Larangam*. Seabird. Wake up."

The old man was already awake, sitting with his back against the beech tree. In the darkness Kaleku had not been able to see him and was startled when it seemed that the tree spoke to him.

"Stop your talking and smell the air," the tree said.

The young man did as he was told.

A dark shadow at the base of the tree detached itself and stood.

The air was heavy with the sickly reek of seaweed. The tides were low and the level of the sea had fallen, pulling back almost to the edge of the reef. Long skeins of bladder wrack were stranded on the slimy coral. For months the seaweed would steam in the hot daytime sun and its salt-sweet putrefaction would hang over the island like a stinking mist. It was the smell of *lamat*.

Old Sea-bird joined the young man. Together they stood looking out over the light-ening lagoon.

"It is the smell of sharks," said Sea-bird. "Let your nose get to know it."

Kaleku nodded.

The day was not far off when he would have to paddle out through the entrance to the lagoon, alone, and go far out into the open sea in search of the shark roads.

The canoe was finished already. He had spent all his spare hours in the long, blustery months of *lavat* making it, chipping and hollowing the ironwood log with the old stone adzes. The work had been slow and difficult, and often he had looked longingly at the glinting steel of the modern axes and chisels that stood in the corner of the hut, wishing he could secretly use them and ease his labor. But he had known that he couldn't. Those tools were for other things, not for the *lesim*. The canoes of Shark Callers could only be made in the way they always had, or disaster would surely accompany them. The other Shark Callers would not have known if he had cheated, but he would have known and would have been ashamed. And he had the uneasy feeling that the sharks would have known, too.

Sea-bird had helped him with the canoe, teaching him how to hollow out the inside so that it was perfectly balanced and to rub the surface with wet coral so that the wood shone white with lime and was as impervious to water as metal.

Together they had cut strong, straight branches for the outrigger supports, stripped the bark from them, and stuck them upright in the sand outside the boy's house to dry. There the wood had remained for many weeks, until Sea-bird was satisfied. Then they bored holes into the sides of the canoe with sharpened bones and lashed the hard supports to the canoe with vine rope, the old man fussing over the knots.

"Tighter. You must lash them tighter," he grumbled.

He shook his head at the carelessness of youth as he fingered the knots Kaleku had tied.

"This canoe will not bring you home," he said, waggling a loose support. "The shark will hear your canoe cry out, and he will know it is not a good canoe. He will break it with one swipe of his tail and that will be the end of Kaleku."

Kaleku smiled. The men of the village, who in their day had also had to suffer Sea-bird's impatience, had warned him what to expect. But he was not offended by the old man's criticisms. This man had hunted sharks all his life and had always come home safely. Others, many others, who had not heeded Sea-bird's wisdom, who had hurried making their canoes and paddles, had not come back at all.

Beyond the sight of land, the sea is very lonely and very deep. The only thing between man and shark is the canoe.

So Kaleku had listened well and was satisfied that he had done all that Sea-bird had asked of him.

Now the time was here. Now Sea-bird would work the magic to prepare him to sail the shark roads. They stood together, the old man and the boy, looking toward the ocean.

And far, far out, sliding silently and with effortless strength along the silver highways of the sea, the sharks waited.

THREE

The engine throbbed gently, making a pretense of reliability that fooled no one. Andy's father cocked his head to one side, listened suspiciously to its note, and muttered darkly under his breath. The engine was an old enemy, and he didn't trust it an inch. Any second now it would wheeze, clang, rattle, cough, and, finally, expire. He hated it with a deep hatred for the years of skinned knuckles, burned fingers, and frayed tempers. Hated it for the countless hours spent lying half upside down in the foul, diesel-smelling water deep in the ship's bilges, trying to coax the recalcitrant monster into life.

Andy smiled.

"Leave it alone, Dad. It'll hear you and stop all the sooner, just to be awkward."

"I know. It's like having a crotchety old aunt living on board, nagging at you all the time and at any minute likely to have an attack of the vapors. I'm not even sure it's worth its weight."

Sally, seated out on *Quintana*'s prow, called back disdainfully. "You two," she said, always the coolly logical one. "You talk about it as though it's alive. It's a *thing*. If you took it out and repaired it properly sometime instead of holding it together with string and tape, it might perform better. And speaking of vapors, is that bacon sandwiches I smell?"

"It is." Mom's voice floated up from the galley. "Bacon sandwiches and tea coming up any second."

"Good," replied Dad. "That will take our minds off the engine for a while. We'll be out of the harbor in about an hour. Perhaps when we get into open sea, there'll be some wind."

Andy groaned to himself. His father had said "perhaps there'll be some wind" with an inflection they all knew very well: the "perhaps pigs will fly" inflection.

Dad was in one of his pessimistic moods, and they would all suffer for it for a few days, until he'd gotten dry land out of his system.

Andy watched his father busying himself with the sails and the gear. Now in his late forties, Peter Thompson looked much older, his hair silvered by years of tropical sun, his face deeply lined and scored by long exposure to the harshest winds on the planet. His painfully thin frame, hovering over his task like a long, brown bird, looked too frail to house the strength they all knew it did. He worked awkwardly, his left shoulder raised slightly and his left arm stiff and twisted. It gave him the appearance of having one arm shorter than the other. Years ago *Quintana* had been broached and had lost one of her masts in massive seas off the African coast. Peter Thompson had been catapulted from the cockpit into the sea. As he dragged himself back on board by his safety line, the flailing mast had caught him a crashing blow to the shoulder and shattered his collarbone. Now he had a faintly comic lopsided bearing, which he would frequently exaggerate to the profound embarrassment of his family.

"Quasimodo" he would mutter when the mood took him, and he would raise his shoulder higher, lean forward, and lope along busy streets, shouting "The bells, the bells," while his family tried to pretend that they did not know him.

But the pattern of life was always the same. The longer they remained on land, the rarer and more spasmodic the high spirits and jokes became.

Andy had long ago realized that his father could not cope with towns and people. He needed the spaces and emptiness of the sea; he needed its unpredictability and its constant movement; he needed, every day, to look out at a new horizon and head for it. Only on the move was he truly happy.

He turned and caught Andy looking at him, then grinned and winked. "Stop daydreaming. You're getting too close to the shore for comfort. It's very shallow in front of Matupit village there. I don't want to spend the first two hours of this voyage digging *Quintana*'s keel out of a sandbank, if you don't mind."

"Sorry."

Andy spun the wheel and watched the prow swing around until he had it centered on the strange needles of rock that rose up from the middle of the harbor, about a mile away. He frowned, his good humor momentarily banished. Just for a while he had forgotten why they were leaving. The rocks, which the people called The Beehives, reminded him. They had risen up from the depths of the harbor floor at the last eruption.

He turned his head back and looked at Matupit village. He had walked through it several times and had even made friends there, of a sort. The fleeting friendships that come of strangeness.

The old, toothless man with the mouth stained bright red from chewing the narcotic betel nut, who had offered him a slice of his precious nut and some lime from his little woven-leaf bag. Andy had tried it, to be polite. He had found it dry and bitter, and it had made his head swim.

The laughing, naked children who had surrounded him and stared and wanted to touch him to see if the white came off his skin.

The giggling, shy girls whose hands had flown to their mouths when he approached and who had disappeared into their huts convulsed with happy embarrassment when he spoke to them.

Tiny friendships, but real, and memorable. Brief encounters, yes. But encounters that had touched his life.

What would happen to those people now?

His eyes drifted up from the village to the volcano. He stared at it with fascination.

Close up, it looked more sinister. Jagged spurs of rock around the crater turned it into a savagely toothed mouth yawning with menace. Great stains of yellow flowed from the rim, where beds of sulfur had settled. Jets of steam and smoke periodically shot from the inner walls and hung briefly on the air before being snatched away, swirling, into the sky.

But there was no sound.

Strangely, this deep, expectant silence added to the threat. It seemed as though the volcano held its breath, waiting for its moment. When would the moment come? Hours, days, weeks? Come it must. Irreversible, the vulcanologists had said. Irreversible. No going back.

Andy looked back down at the village. So their moment would come, too. It was only a matter of time. Their homes would be destroyed, their way of life ended at this place forever.

What if the experts got it wrong and the volcano took them by surprise? The last senior vulcanologist, here in this very town, had been killed only a few years ago by a surprise *nuee ardente* while he was on the slopes. So, even for the experts, there was always that terrifying unpredictability, that "one in a million" chance.

Andy shut out the thought. It was too horrible to think of what might happen. And there was no point. What would happen, would happen.

He dragged his eyes away from the village and closed his mind to it. Then he spun the wheel back a little, correcting *Quintana*'s course. Less than an hour now and they would be out in open sea and speeding away. Perhaps, in a few weeks' time, in another part of the Pacific, he would read what had happened here.

He settled down to eat the sandwich that had arrived, as if by magic, at his side. He had been so preoccupied with his thoughts that he had not even noticed his mother bringing it to him.

Keeping his eye firmly on the harbor entrance, he guided the ship quietly away from Rabaul. Gradually the volcano slid past and was replaced by another gentler cone, the less threatening Rabalankaia. Finally, the beautiful grassed cone of the long-dormant South Daughter slipped past them on their port side, and they were out into the open Bismarck Sea.

Peter Thompson's pessimism about the wind proved to be well founded. There was no wind at all. The sea was flat, as calm as it had been in the harbor.

"Damn. I knew it. Somehow I knew it. I had a feeling about this trip. It's going to be one of those trips where everything goes wrong."

Andy sighed and grinned.

Sally groaned and said, "Yes, Dad," in a voice heavy with resignation and sarcasm.

Mom put her head out from the cabin. "In thirty years of traveling with your father, I have never heard him begin any trip to anywhere without the words 'It's going to be one of those trips where everything goes wrong.' One day I'll throw him overboard."

"We'll help you."

Peter Thompson scowled. "You'll see. You mark my words."

At that moment the engine coughed loudly and expired.

Nobody dared say anything.

There was complete silence as Peter Thompson, face set hard, descended silently into the bowels of *Quintana*.

Another voyage had begun.

Four hours later, Dr. David Lowenstein, chief vulcanologist, telephoned Inspector Paul Songo, head of Rabaul's police. His message was brief:

"The seismographs are picking up increased activity. There's no great urgency. I don't want any panic, so we won't sound the siren. I think, however, that there is a good chance that Matupi will go critical in the next few days."

"Red Alert?" asked the chief inspector.

"Red Alert. Begin the evacuation."

FOUR

ౘ

Old Sea-bird and Kaleku spent the final day in making the *larung* with which to call the sharks and the *kasaman* with which to snare them.

Kaleku collected four of the biggest coconuts he could find and took them to the husking pole. Quickly and skillfully, he drove each one down on the spike, stripping away the fibrous husks and revealing the shells. He broke the coconuts into perfectly even halves, removed the white flesh, and left the empty shells to dry in the sun while he went to find a strip of bamboo for the hoop.

Meanwhile Sea-bird had brought a thick log about four feet in length and was sitting quietly in front of his house, chipping at it with an adze. He was making the *kasaman* himself, for this, the propeller-shaped snare, was the most important part of Kaleku's equipment and he could not trust the young novice to make it himself.

Kaleku returned with the bamboo, collected the half coconut shells, and sat down beside the old man. Taking up a knife, he bored a hole into the first of the shells and threaded it onto the strip of bamboo.

Old Sea-bird eyed him suspiciously, then reached out and inspected the shells and the bamboo. He ran his fingers along the edges where the shells had been split and flexed the bamboo strip, testing its suppleness.

Kaleku waited for him to criticize, but things must have met with Sea-bird's approval, for he simply grunted, then turned back to his own work.

Kaleku continued to thread the shells in the way he had been taught, some back to back, some with their open ends facing each other. When all eight were threaded, he tied the ends of the bamboo strip together so that he now had a large hoop on which the coconut shells moved freely. He stood and tested it, giving it a vigorous shake. The shells made a surprisingly loud clacking noise that echoed back from the palm trees behind Sea-bird's house.

Kaleku smiled, pleased that the rattle was so effective.

Sea-bird nodded and grinned. "Good," he said. "But you must do it like this."

He stood and took the rattle from Kaleku. He held it by his side and gave two quick flicks of his wrist.

Clack-clack, clack-clack went the rattle.

"See how it calls," said Sea-bird. "It is calling '*Shark come. Shark come.*' Only if you do it this way will the *lembe* hear it and come to you."

He shook the rattle again, and Kaleku could hear the words in the rhythmic banging of the shells.

"Shark come. Shark come."

He looked out to sea. For a moment he was apprehensive. Here, on land, it was all easy. Out there, alone on the shark roads, how would he fare as he plunged the *larung* into the sea beside his tiny, frail canoe and called that great, easy strength from the depths of the ocean?

"Why does the *lembe* come?" he asked. "What does he think the sound is?"

"Ah, that no one knows," Sea-bird replied. "The Spirit, Moroa, first taught man to make the rattle in the Spirit-time. No one knows now what the shark thinks the *larung* is. But when it is shaken in the water of the shark roads, the sound will travel many miles outward. Whatever the shark thinks, he is curious and always comes. Perhaps he hears fish jumping or birds diving into the water. And there is the magic. Without the magic you may shake the *larung* from now until the end of time and the shark will not come. But it is not yet time for the magic. First we will finish the *kasaman*."

The log was already cut into a rough propeller shape and now needed only to be smoothed. Then a hole could be cut into its center and the vine rope threaded through to form the noose that would snare the shark.

"See," said the old man. "This piece of wood will decide your success or failure. Remember, when you have slipped the noose over the shark's head, you may have to follow him for many miles. He will be angry and will try to shake the *kasaman* off. If you have made it well and have used good rope for the noose, eventually it will tire him so that he can swim no more. Then he is yours."

He handed the wooden blade to Kaleku, and the young man sat down and began to shave the roughness of the wood with the sharp edge of a shell. Again he began to feel a foreboding.

He had no real fear of sharks. A child of this village grew up with the sea and was taught to swim before he could walk. Early in life he had learned that most of the ocean's occupants are concerned with nothing except their own lives. In the sea, human beings are irrelevant. The vivid sea snakes whose deadly venom is as powerful as their colors will retreat into their holes in the reef as a swimmer's shadow passes over them. The great rays, the conger eels, the groupers, though of fearsome appearance, are docile grazers who will quickly vanish if a strange shape enters their territory.

Even sharks, familiar visitors to the reef, cause little alarm. The reef swarms with a million brightly colored morsels more tempting than man. And though people treat sharks with respect and are careful not to spear fish when they are near, in case the frantic thrashing and the smell of blood should bring the sharks to investigate, they are not afraid.

But this, of course, was different. This time Kaleku had to confront the shark. Confront it. Snare it. And kill it.

Alone in a tiny canoe, far from land, far from help, in the silent ocean, he had to do battle with the sea's most fearful, most silently lethal inhabitant.

He looked anxiously out to sea, trying to imagine what he would do when the moment came and the shark answered his call.

Old Sea-bird noticed the boy's uncertain gaze and read his mind.

He sighed heavily and his pale eyes became opaque with memory. He was transported back sixty years to when he had first set out on that daunting journey to the shark roads. He remembered clearly, even after more than half a century, how he had felt on that first day. The sickness of fear in the stomach as he paddled out. The shock as the first great black fin had risen silently out of the sea, only a few feet away from his canoe. The terror as the head had lifted above the flat surface and the single, mercilessly malign eye had fixed itself upon him. And the struggle. The debilitating struggle that had followed.

He had been hours luring the shark into the snare. It had circled and circled, deeply suspicious of the bait fish on the end of the pole. But he had persevered, willing the great creature to come forward. Finally he succeeded. Hunger overcoming its suspicion, the shark had suddenly lurched toward him to take the fish and had slipped into the rope noose of the *kasaman*. With a quick twist of the propeller, Sea-bird had drawn the noose tight about the shark's neck.

But that had only been the beginning. Then had come the chase.

The shark had dived the moment it felt the strange object around its neck. Sea-bird had not been worried. He had known that the light wood of the *kasaman* would bring the shark to the surface as soon as it began to tire. He had just waited and watched.

When the propeller had surfaced and Sea-bird could see it glinting in the sun, it was half a mile away and he had had to give chase, paddling furiously to catch up with it.

And as he had approached, arms breaking with effort, it had vanished down into the depths again, only to resurface another half a mile away.

Old Sea-bird shook his head and sighed as he remembered.

Kaleku looked at him inquiringly. "What, old man? What is it?"

"Nothing. Only an old man's foolish memories. Nothing." He turned his head away from the sea and started to walk back toward his house.

It was a story he did not want to relate, for the memory was too painful. The chase had lasted three days and had taken him to the point of exhaustion, where he was unsure whether he was still alive.

At the end of the third day, just when he thought the shark had finally run out of strength, it had made one last desperate dive to try to shake free of the deadly noose. The rope had given way, and when Sea-bird had next caught sight of the floating *kasaman*, the shark was gone.

Even now, sixty years later, Sea-bird could taste the bitterness of disappointment in his mouth.

"What is wrong, old man?" called Kaleku after him.

"Hush your noise," Sea-bird snapped irritably. "Get on with your work. Finish smoothing your *kasaman*. It must be finished by dusk."

"Do we make the magic tonight?"

"Yes, tonight we make the magic. Tomorrow you go. Finish your work."

And he disappeared into his hut.

In the long, heat-laden afternoon, Sea-bird slept and dreamed of sharks and of shark magic.

Kaleku patiently smoothed his *kasaman*, and when he judged that the demanding old man would be satisfied with it, he laid it to one side. Then he simply sat and waited, looking out over the sea.

Clouds were beginning to gather in the distance. Kaleku was comforted by them. Kumotak, the rainmaker, was already at work. Before dawn there would be rain to flatten the long, rolling swells that drove relentlessly up through the channel between New Ireland and New Britain. His journey to the shark roads would be made easier.

There was only one small interruption to his solitary vigil. Late in the afternoon, when the sun began to sink slowly into the ocean, Kaleku felt the ground beneath him begin to shake.

It was almost imperceptible, a tiny vibration. It lasted only a few seconds, then stopped.

Kaleku gave it no more than a passing thought. But then *guria*s, earthquakes, were so common here that no one would have remarked on it anyway.

FIVE

&&

The engine had been very stubborn.

Quintana had drifted idly at the mouth of the harbor for several hours while Peter Thompson lay in the bilges, surrounded by mechanical parts at which he periodically shouted. The clang of wrenches mingled with curses gave notice that by nightfall he would be in a gale-force temper.

By about three o'clock the ship had floated gently in to shore. Andy kept a careful lookout for rocks and had to pole *Quintana* past a few. Eventually they drifted into the lee of South Daughter, and when Andy was able to judge that they were in about thirty feet of water, he dropped anchor.

So that was the first day's voyage—about five miles.

Or, looked at another way, about two miles away from the volcano, Matupi.

There was nothing to be done about that

anyway. Even if they had known about the Red Alert they couldn't have moved *Quintana*.

"Isn't Submarine Base just along from here?" asked Sally, who was stretched out on top of the doghouse, reading a magazine.

"Yes, just around that little spit of land there."

Sally glanced at her watch. "Half past three. About three hours of light left. Fancy a dive?"

Submarine Base was a place they had visited many times during their stay in Rabaul. Andy had found a reference to it in a book about the Japanese occupation of New Guinea during the Second World War, and he clearly remembered the day he had gone out to investigate.

It had not been easy to find, but the report had described a small white-sanded lagoon locked in by two rocky spits of land with high cliffs at each end. The search was narrowed by the white sand. The sand on most of the beaches of New Britain was volcanic and as black as coal.

Wandering through the villages on the

north coast of the island, he had eventually found a friendly Tolai who knew where the lagoon was and took him there.

In his mind he had expected to find buildings. "Submarine Base" conjured up pictures of huge naval cranes and wharfs and ammunition sheds. So initially he had been very disappointed when he had been led into the cove. There was nothing there at all, just a blindingly white coral-sanded beach and a small lagoon.

But his disappointment had turned to fascination when the Tolai explained.

"The Japanese submarine fleet used to moor here. Hundreds of them at a time, the old men say."

"Here?" asked Andy, incredulous. "It's too small. There isn't room."

The Tolai smiled. "Come," he said. "I will show you. Can you swim?"

Andy had been swimming since he was eighteen months old.

"Yes," he replied, "I can swim."

The Tolai walked into the water and began to stride out into the sea. "Be careful where you put your feet. Watch out for black sea urchins. Their spines are so sharp they will go through the soles of your shoes. If you get one of those in your foot, your leg will swell like an elephant's."

Andy followed him into the water and found that they were walking on the flat top of a coral reef. It was pitted with holes and very sharp, so the walking was difficult. He had to peer into the water at each step and place his feet carefully. The ground dropped away gradually until, when they were thigh deep in the water, it leveled out.

"Just a little farther," said the Tolai.

They had walked perhaps only twenty yards from the shore when the Tolai held out his arm for Andy to stop.

"Now," he said. "Swim forward and look down."

Andy slid down into the water and pushed off with his feet. The surface of the coral was only about three feet below him. The water was absolutely clear, and he could see tiny, brilliantly colored fish nibbling the seaweed growing out of the reef. He kicked a couple of times with his feet and glided a little farther forward.

Without any warning whatsoever the sea-bed abruptly vanished, and Andy emerged out over the edge of the reef. If his face had not been under the water, he would have gasped with shock. For a brief moment his mind spun with vertigo. One second he had been in three feet of warm, inviting water, the coral below him so close he could reach down and touch it. The next he was out over the edge of a vast coral cliff that plummeted down, down, down to fearful depths. If there had been time for logic, he would have known that he couldn't fall. He was swimming. But his brain didn't give him any time. The shock was too sudden, too great. Without any rational thought at all, instinct for survival spun him around in the water and with two frantic strokes he was back in the shallows and standing, gasping, beside the Tolai.

The man grinned.

Andy spluttered with a mixture of annoyance and embarrassment. "Why didn't you warn me?"

"The first moment is the best. Anyway, if you'd gotten into trouble I would have hauled you out."

"It's incredible, absolutely incredible. I've dived on hundreds of reefs. I've never seen anything like this one."

"I know. Go back again, now you know what to expect, and take another look."

Andy took a deep breath, slid down into the water, and pushed himself off. A couple of strokes and he was out over the rim of the reef. This time, without the unexpectedness, he was able to take in what he saw. He was over a huge coral amphitheater. The walls curved away from him to the left and right beyond the limits of his sight. Looking down the sheer sides of the precipices, he found that the brilliant white light of the surface melted into a pale, translucent green, then, lower, to ice blue, then to a deep azure. Finally, hundreds of feet down, the rock was swallowed in profound, disturbing blackness.

For a second he recoiled from the unknown, unspeakable things the blackness might contain. Quickly he drew his eyes back up again and looked outward into the amphitheater. The sight took his breath away. The great sea bowl teemed with life. Iridescent shoals of emerald, ruby, and sapphire fish performed elegant ballets. Brilliant yellow-and-black butterfly cod flapped like bright birds through the water. Tiny pinpoints of colored light darted in and out of the swaying sea anemones that clung to the rock walls. From every crack and hole in the coral, faces stared out: clowns' masks of blue and red here; ferocious, nightmare monsters there. About fifty feet down, its head protruding an inch or two from his lair, Andy could see an enormous grouper, a fish so ugly it made him shudder, but one he knew to be harmless and shy. A few feet out from him a conger eel slithered menacingly by, its jaws open in anticipation of a tasty catch.

And farther out, sliding slowly and with infinite grace, like gray ghosts on the margins of his vision, he could discern the menacing outlines of a group of nurse sharks.

He returned to the shallows and stood once more beside the Tolai.

"Thank you for bringing me. It's too much to take in at one go. I'll leave it for today and come back with my gear tomorrow."

"Okay."

"I can see why the Japanese used it. It must be one of the deepest reefs in the islands. A perfect hiding place."

"Yes, they used to moor just out there, sometimes hundreds of them at once. A tanker ship would come around from the harbor and refuel the submarines at night. They would surface two or three at a time, then move on. They were going south, down through The Slot to Honiara. The really big battles took place down there."

Andy looked out again, trying to imagine the scene, the hushed but urgent bustling as the sinister, gunmetal gray craft surfaced silently in the night. It seemed hard to believe that the savagery of the war had touched this peaceful, beautiful place.

Over the next weeks he had returned many times—with Sally, his constant companion, and his mother and father when they had been able—and explored the endless variety of this magical place. Gradually some of the more curious of its denizens had become friends.

The big, ugly grouper had soon learned that these strange creatures would bring tasty tidbits. Before long he was deigning to emerge a few inches from his hole and feed from their hands. Evil-looking congers would come to investigate them and swim in and out of their legs, rubbing themselves against them like cats. Now and then a lone dolphin would lollop into the arena and show off for them shamelessly, twisting and leaping, vanishing down into the deep blackness and then roaring up again, scattering the more nervous fish away.

"Hello, is there anyone at home? I said, 'Do you fancy a dive?' "

"Sorry, Sal. I was lost for a minute there. I was remembering the first time I found the place."

"Well, remember on the way. You're wasting daylight. Are we going or what?"

"Yes, of course. You get the scuba gear. I'll pull the dinghy around."

Sally jumped down into the cockpit and disappeared into the cabin to bring out the diving gear. By the time she had emerged with the first pair of tanks, Andy had pulled the dinghy alongside. They loaded the equipment and set off.

"Take care," shouted Mom. "And be back before dark."

"It's all right for some," came a plaintive cry from somewhere in the depths of

Quintana. Followed by "Enjoy yourselves, won't you," heavy with sarcasm.

Sally got ready while Andy rowed. It took only a few minutes to round the headland and be in the lagoon, so by the time they were anchoring at the edge of the reef, Sally had her weighted belt, tanks, and flippers already on. Andy carefully checked her tanks, then donned his equipment, too. They washed their face masks in the sea to stop them from misting up, then sat one on each side of the dinghy with their backs to the sea.

"One. Two. Three," Andy mumbled through his mouthpiece.

Simultaneously on "Three," they both fell backward over the side and into the water. Andy swam around the dinghy until he had Sally in sight, then gave her the "thumbs down" sign to descend.

Together they sank slowly down the sides of the precipice.

The fear that they had both first experienced had long ago departed, and now what had been daunting and sinister merely seemed warm and friendly. They were glad to be here and glad that circumstance had given them this one final, unexpected chance to say good-bye.

Sally headed immediately down to the old grouper, who, as always, was contemplating the world from his lair. She settled in the water in front of him, and recognizing her, he emerged a little way to have his head stroked.

Andy swam out, away from the reef. He wanted to take a last look at the whole of it, to take in the entire huge curved bowl with its million strange inhabitants. A last mental photograph, which he could carry with him forever. He swam very strongly and was soon several hundred yards out.

Then he stopped, turned, and simply lay motionless in the water, happy to stare and let the movement and color of it all wash over him. No matter how many times he had been here, he had never tired of this sight. He let his eyes drift from side to side. Between the lazily drifting shoals of fish, he could see the bright scarlet of Sally's bikini and the silver of her air tanks as she quietly said good-bye to her friend.

Then, almost imperceptibly at first, something began to happen. Andy rubbed his mask, thinking that some misting on the glass was blurring his vision. But it wasn't that. The strange sensation remained. It seemed as though the reef, all of it, this vast million tons of coral, was shaking. Vibrating.

He shook his head sharply, hoping to clear it. It couldn't be the reef. It must be him. He hadn't dived for a few days, so the pressure on his ears had made him a little light-headed, a little out of balance. Yes, that was it. But it didn't work. The vibration seemed to be getting stronger.

A sudden chill of fear ran through him, momentarily paralyzing him. It *was* moving. The whole reef was moving, trembling as though shaken by a giant hand. He threw off the fear instantly.

Sally! he screamed in his mind. *Sally. Get away!*

He began to swim with all the strength of panic toward her.

Things took on the terrible air of a slow-motion nightmare. He seemed to be swimming through molasses, traveling dreadfully, painfully, slowly. Sally wouldn't know what was happening. She was too close to the rock to be able to see.

The shaking was increasing, and Andy was terrified that the rocks would begin to crumble, to fall and crush her.

Then, suddenly, incredibly, everything else was on the move, too. The great shoals of fish whirled agitatedly for a second or two and then began to teem away from the reef toward the open sea. From a distance he saw with horror the great grouper shoot out from his hole, knocking Sally sideways as though she were a rag doll. A long stream of bubbles rose up violently from close by her head.

Andy went cold. The fish had either knocked her mouthpiece out of her mouth or severed her breathing tube. He swam even harder, fighting his way through the multitudes of fleeing fish.

Momentarily Sally's hands went up to her head, as though she had been hurt, then she began to rise. Kicking hard, she shot upward toward the surface.

Andy didn't lessen his speed but was relieved to see her going up. She was obviously not too hurt. He started to rise, too, angling himself upward so that he would surface at the reef edge and join Sally.

The reef stopped shaking as suddenly as it had started. It was all over. It hadn't lasted more than a few seconds but had seemed, in the urgency of danger, to have taken hours.

In the last few feet before he surfaced, Andy looked down. He shivered, partly from the reaction of his fear, partly from the unearthly eeriness of what he now saw.

The reef, the entire great caldron, was deserted. Every living thing was gone. A million creatures had vanished as though they had never been. It was a scene from another planet, a desolate planet that had never known life.

Then he surfaced into the sun and found Sally sitting in the shallow water at the reef's edge, ruefully nursing her bruised head.

"The clumsy great fool," she said. "He came out of that hole like a bullet. Knocked me flying. Knocked my mouthpiece out. He could have killed me. What a way to say good-bye."

"You're all right, then?"

" 'Course I'm all right, stupid. Would I be sitting here talking to you if I wasn't all right? And I thought I heard a roaring or something. Did you see anything?"

"There was an earth tremor, I think. The reef was shaking. You couldn't see. You were too close. That's what startled the grouper. It startled everything else, too. Everything has gone. It's deserted down there now."

Sally went silent and stared down over the edge. "Everything?" she asked finally, wonderingly.

"Everything."

Sally shivered. "Let's get back now," she said. "I think Dad ought to know about this."

"Right."

Sally stood and turned, looking inshore at the steeply rising bulk of South Daughter. "Matupi's just behind here, isn't it?"

"Yes."

"Do you think it's started?"

"How would I know a thing like that?"

"They say that animals know more about the world than us. They say they can predict earthquakes and eruptions. The forest always goes silent just before an earthquake. Perhaps these fish know something's going to happen."

"Nonsense," replied Andy. "Those are just old wives' tales. Let's get back to

Quintana. That bang on the head has made you silly. It was just the tremor that startled them, that's all. Everything will drift back shortly. Let's go home."

Sally pondered the surface of the water for a moment or two in silence. "Mmm," she said finally. "Perhaps you're right." She started loading the diving gear into the dinghy.

"Of course I'm right. Get in and let's get out of here."

They climbed into the boat, and Andy began to row steadily away from Submarine Base back to the safety of *Quintana.*

"Of course I'm right," Andy repeated to himself as they rowed away.

But he was secretly praying that *Quintana*'s engine would be repaired by the time they got back and that he could persuade his father to leave immediately.

The sudden exodus of life had been too shocking, too precipitous. Small earthquakes happened all the time here. Everything, creatures and people alike, was used to them.

No, this was different. Sally was right. The creatures did know. This was a warning. And it was up to the people to take heed.

SIX

Old Sea-bird led the way inland toward the island's center.

He carried a torch made of reeds soaked in fish oil and bound tightly. It burned slowly with a small, flickering flame. Faint moonlight seeped through the clouds, but the coconut palms were planted densely here and their huge leaves blocked out much of the light. The flames from the torch bounced eerily back from the tall black trunks. To Kaleku's nervous eyes it seemed as though the trees moved, stepping forward to inspect them as they approached and receding as they passed.

They were on their way to the Shark Stone. The time for the magic had come.

Kaleku found it difficult to keep up. For all his age, Sea-bird moved more nimbly than the boy in the darkness. It was a journey he had done a thousand times. Familiarity guided his feet, melting him through the trees. Kaleku, tripping and stumbling on exposed roots and fallen coconuts, sometimes lost sight of him and found himself hurrying through the haphazard maze of black tree trunks, following only a winking light. It felt unreal, as though he followed a spirit firefly.

He was eager to see the Shark Stone.

He knew of it, of course, and had heard its voice a hundred times. It was there in his earliest memories, though the *tambu* had forbidden him to see it until the time was right.

He remembered, as a small child, waking in the dead hours of night and lying shivering in his bed as the strange, booming cry rattled through the trees behind his hut. It had a deep, elemental resonance, like the groan of the earth when the *guria*s came. It shook the thin walls of the huts and agitated the high palm tree fronds so that they rattled together like dry bones clicking in the night.

And, hearing it, all the villagers of the island would know that Old Sea-bird was at his magic, and that tomorrow a Shark Caller's canoe would be missing from the beach.

So Kaleku had grown up with the knowledge of the Shark Stone, its night calls a constant reminder that one day, when his time came, it would be his canoe that was gone.

Now he was to see it, and he knew that his heart was thumping not just from the exertion of trying to keep up with Sea-bird.

The ground began to slope upward. They had reached the center of the island and were beginning to climb the volcano they called Sinali.

"Now we approach," said the old man. "Tread softly so you do not awake Sinali, or he will burn us with fire."

The volcano had long been dormant, and Kaleku was too young to have seen it last erupt. To Sea-bird the memory was still vivid.

"Back in the *tumbuna* time, the time of the spirits, Aruako, the first of the great shark hunters, fell in love with the Moon Woman, whose face he saw in the sea. She loved him in return, but she was promised to Sinali, the Sun Man. When Sinali saw that Aruako and the Moon Woman were lovers, he flew into a rage and hurled a ball of fire down from the sun to destroy their home.

So fierce was the fire that it melted the earth underneath their house, right down to the center of the world. Sinali banished Aruako and the Moon Woman to the sea forever. That is why the spirit of Aruako calls sharks on the seas, with the Moon Woman floating in the water beside him. Sometimes Sinali gets suspicious and thinks they are trying to return to land, so he releases his fire from the earth to warn them. It is fearful to see. Tread quietly."

They were up above the palm trees now and the pale moon painted a cold, hard light onto the mountainside. Here the landscape was harsh and forbidding. Stunted trees dotted the slopes, their hideously twisted arms reaching silently up to the stars.

Kaleku turned and looked out to sea. The Moon Woman floated on the surface of the whispering ocean and Kaleku shivered a little as he thought of the *masalai,* the spirit of Aruako, sailing his canoe forever beside her.

"Look up and you will see their children, Kukwana and Didigar, the morning and evening stars, who guide their parents about the seas. Take note of them; they will guide you, too."

They were traversing the side of the volcano, about a hundred feet below the rim. Kaleku was breathing heavily, but the climb seemed not to have affected the old man at all.

"Nearly there," said Sea-bird.

Kaleku followed without answering. The ground felt hot beneath his bare feet. He thought of the fires raging deep below him and hoped Sinali did not hear their footsteps.

The path wound in and out of huge lava folds in the side of the volcano, so that sometimes they turned into profoundly black crevices, only to emerge again into light. Eventually they arrived at a deep bowl in the rock where a huge air bubble had petrified the molten lava into a perfectly circular depression. Here the moonlight was so angled that it flooded into the hollow.

Old Sea-bird continued walking without pause, but Kaleku stopped for a moment to take in the scene.

The floor of the bowl was flat and

covered with a deep layer of pumice dust. As Sea-bird walked, his feet sank into the dust and small clouds swirled around his ankles. It made him look strangely ethereal, as though he floated across the ground on a mist.

He was heading for the center of the bowl.

Here another air bubble, deep underground, had pushed up the lava to form a circular raised platform about twenty feet across. It was so perfectly formed that it could have been carved and polished by humans. Leaning against it, to the left, was a huge ironwood club, the size of a man but cut in exactly the shape of the clubs the Shark Callers carried with them in their canoes.

The Shark Stone, whose great voice Kaleku had heard through all the years of his growing, was here in front of him.

But his eyes were drawn across the surface of the stone to its right-hand edge. There, resting on its bed of human bones, was the great *masalai* shark. Carved centuries ago by the first of the Shark Callers, from the hard volcanic rock of the island, its surface gleamed blackly. Its body was curved slightly, as though it was in motion, and Kaleku could almost see the great supple muscles rippling in the stone of its back. Its dorsal fin, that black awesome sail that for man is the very essence of shark, was etched, clearly and terrifyingly, against the lighter rock of the walls of the hollow.

Kaleku found that his hands were trembling a little at the terrible, easy power that flowed from the great stone beast, and he held them tightly to his sides to steady them. Then his eyes came to rest on the head.

The shark was looking out to sea, its stone eyes fixed on a point far, far out on the long, lonely shark roads, where its spirit moved eternally through vast distances and incomprehensible depths.

Its great carved mouth was open, the jaws widely stretched.

Kaleku's eyes remained long and wonderingly on the mouth. It was like a huge man-trap, ready to snap shut with a strength and ferocity that would remove a man's leg or arm with the ease of a child biting through a blade of grass. Into the stone the carvers had placed the teeth of a long-dead shark. The ivory winked light back to him, and the shadows playing on the shark's mouth made phantom bloodstains on the teeth and lips.

Kaleku had to tell himself that this great, terrible shark was only stone, an effigy, unable to move.

But there, high on the volcano, in this place surrounded by mystery and magic, it was hard to convince himself.

The old man had arrived at the side of the platform. He turned and signaled for Kaleku to join him. "Now," he said. "Sit, and we will begin."

Kaleku did as he was ordered. He sat cross-legged on the dusty ground and waited.

Sea-bird climbed onto the platform, bent over the edge, and hauled up the heavy club. Dragging it to the center of the rock, he stood, feet apart, holding the club upright in front of him.

"First we call the ancestors back from the *tumbuna* time. Without the *masalai* of the old ones, no man can call a shark."

Then he raised the heavy club a few inches from the surface of the stone and let it drop. There was a dull thud of wood on stone, a small sound only. But it was followed seconds later by an echo deep in the ground. Kaleku felt it reverberate beneath him. The platform was hollow underneath.

Before the echo could die, Sea-bird raised the club and dropped it again, catching the echo and augmenting it with another dull surface thud. A second echo joined the first and the rumble from below became higher pitched and louder. Gradually Sea-bird began to increase speed, raising and dropping the club rhythmically onto the rock.

Thud. Thud. Thud. Thud. Thud.

The sound beneath began to grow and grow. Trapped in the great rock caverns beneath them, it sought escape and seeped out into the long tunnels that ran, like veins, throughout the volcano's cone. Echo tumbled onto echo, roaring through the channels below like a great wind.

Then, finally, the sound began to emerge from its captivity. High above them, from a narrow, long-dead steam vent near Sinali's rim, it screamed out furiously into the night air. The narrowness of the exit squeezed it, magnified and distilled it, so that it emerged as a huge roar.

The sound of thunder, of whirlwind and storm.

Kaleku shook his head in wonder.

The sound was so great it would indeed wake the *masalai,* wake the dead.

Sea-bird began to conjure them.

Names of the great Shark Callers from across the centuries were called out into the night, each name followed by a soft hiss.

The hiss of a snake. Or of Pilai, the lizard.

"Manu. *Sssssss . . .*"

"Kukutak. *Sssssss . . .*"

"Bunag. *Sssssss . . .*"

"Kendi. Honbain. Tura."

"Kumotak. Mangon. Sido."

The names rolled back over the generations. Back to Kabinana and Karvuvu, the first of the Shark Callers and the sons of Mother Earth.

Sea-bird stopped his hammering of the rock. The echoes rolled away into the depths, and the sound began to fade. Eventually the roaring became a dull rumble, then a whisper, then died away into silence.

Silence.

Kaleku waited. The old man stood stock-still on the platform.

Minutes passed.

Then, below them on the slopes of the volcano came a soft sound from the trees. The hair began to stand up on the back of Kaleku's neck and on his arms. He shivered slightly. A soft, insistent rustling rose from deep in the forested slopes: the sound of slow, slow feet dragging along the ground.

Sea-bird hissed. "Come, Pilai, come," he murmured.

Kaleku turned and watched. At the base of the treeline the shadows twisted and folded. Slowly they began to detach themselves and take form, creeping shadows, emerging from holes and lairs deep in the ground. First one, then two, then ten, then twenty, from every direction they advanced. Their grotesque serpent heads moved from side to side in a strange, jerky motion, forked tongues whipping out and back again, exploring the air.

The boy felt instant revulsion. These great, ugly creatures he loathed more than any other living thing. Even snakes frightened him less than these huge lizards. They seemed unearthly, monstrous; stranded by a cruel trick of time in a world where they had no place, a world where they lurked forever in dark holes, hiding their ugliness.

"Come, Pilai, come," repeated Sea-bird.

He climbed down from the platform and signaled Kaleku to join him at the edge of the hollow.

Kaleku rose and went across to the old man. He watched with horrified fascination as the monitors advanced. They were still emerging from the trees, their numbers increasing all the time, swelling into a river of cold flesh. Their strange, automaton sway added to the horror.

The first of the lizards reached the stone platform and began to climb. Its claws slipped and screeched on the smooth rock, but it gained slow and painful purchase here and there, inching its way upward. The rest of the creatures followed gradually, until the whole platform disappeared under a seething reptilian mass. The stone shark was swallowed beneath them as they flowed over it. Hissing and spitting filled the air, and as they reached the far side of the platform,

Kaleku could hear the soft, sickening thuds as they dropped onto the ground on the other side.

They began to ascend toward the rim of the volcano.

Sea-bird waited until the flow was coming to an end and the last of the lizards was past the shark.

"So," he whispered to Kaleku. "It has begun."

He started toward the platform again.

"Pilai, the keeper of the *masalai,* has done his work. The sharks will know. Pilai has taken the spirit of the shark and now climbs with it. He has come out of his hole and climbs. So now the sharks in the ocean will be climbing, too. Tomorrow they will be at the surface of the sea, just as Pilai climbs to the top of the land."

Kaleku nodded. In the depths the sharks would be stirring.

He looked again at the great stone shark. The two curved rows of teeth gleamed in the moonlight.

"Come," said Sea-bird. "There is one last thing to do."

He picked up his palm-leaf basket from

beside the Shark Stone and took out a short piece of heavy vine. He handled it carefully, for the vine was covered with tiny, needle-sharp thorns.

"Here," he said, handing the vine to Ka-leku. "Rub this on the shark's teeth. The thorns will scrape his teeth and set them on edge. It will make him think of food, of crunching bones. Then tomorrow, when you shake your *larung* in the sea, he will come to you quickly."

Kaleku took the vine from him and walked across to the shark. As he rubbed the vine across the teeth, Sea-bird stood silent, looking out to sea.

The thorns rasped harshly across the teeth.

Sea-bird nodded his approval.

"That will do," he said. "The shark feels it."

He was well satisfied with his magic. He could see the shark roads in his mind. The sharks were rising. He could feel them. He turned back to Kaleku.

"Everything is ready. The sharks will be waiting for you. When it is light you go."

Kaleku nodded.

He joined the old man, and for a few moments they stood together gazing at the sea, each with his own thoughts. Then they turned away, gathered their things, and set off down the hillside.

As they left the hollow, Kaleku glanced back at the shark one final time.

He thought, just for a moment, that he caught a glimpse of red on its teeth. A small bolt of fear rippled through his body, but he quickly controlled it. It was nothing. Only the shadows tricking him as they had done before.

But later, reaching out his hand to steady himself on his descent, he found that his hand was bleeding. A thorn had lodged itself in his flesh.

The blood on the teeth of the shark was his.

SEVEN

۶۱۶

Sally told her father of the strange occurrence at the reef as soon as they got back.

"Hmm," he said. "Very interesting. The sooner we get out of here the better."

Ann Thompson glowered at her husband. "Oh, for goodness' sake," she snapped, afraid he would cause the children alarm. "If anything critical was happening, the vulcanologists would have raised the alarm."

"We wouldn't necessarily hear it. We're miles away."

"Perhaps. But we'd be seeing some activity," she continued, trying to divert him. "There'd be boats coming out, planes taking off. Something would be happening."

"I'd rather put my faith in fish than scientists."

"I never thought I'd hear a doctor say that," Andy chipped in.

"I've seen too many things that science can't explain, doctor or not," his father retorted. "I've seen perfectly healthy Aboriginals lie down and die simply because they've been cursed, had 'the bone' pointed at them. Find an explanation for that."

"That's not the same thing at all. That's people. People can convince themselves they're going to die, so they do."

"It's all right, Mom," Sally said, realizing why her mother was arguing. "I've made up my mind anyway. Creatures are closer to the earth than we are. They know."

"Quite right," said Peter Thompson. "And I've wasted enough time already. Back to the engine."

He disappeared down into the bilges.

In their hearts everyone was in agreement, but human nature balks at looming disaster, preferring to make excuses, hoping that the worst will not happen. But they all knew. They had all had nights when they had suddenly found themselves awake and wondering what had wakened them, realizing eventually that it had been the silence. Earthquakes never come unannounced. The singing of the crickets and cicadas stills; the tree frogs cease their booming croak; the fruit bats stop their bickering. Then, moments later, the village dogs begin to howl in anguish. And all of this minutes before the needles of the delicate seismographs begin to record the first tremors. All the computers, the instruments, the most up-to-date technology on earth are no match for the creatures.

That was why Peter Thompson worked feverishly throughout the evening, stripping down components, cleaning and examining them, reassembling them when he was satisfied. Periodically he would press the starter. The engine would cough and turn over obediently, but would not fire. And, cursing, he would start again.

Finally, just before midnight, he was about to admit defeat. Then, dismantling the fuel pump for the fourth time, he noticed a tiny pinhole in the diaphragm.

"Got it," he muttered to himself. He guessed that the hole was sucking in air and not enough fuel was getting to the engine.

He replaced the diaphragm, bolted the pump back onto the engine, and pressed the starter. The engine turned, coughed, gave a halfhearted lurch or two, but still did not start.

Peter Thompson swore.

"Come on. Come on," he snarled.

He pressed the starter again. The same thing happened, but this time the engine coughed three or four times in quick succession.

"There's a girl, you're trying, aren't you. Come on now. This time."

Once more he pushed hard on the starter button.

The engine clattered and spluttered, then miraculously burst into life. Hesitant at first, its note quickly became more even until, finally, a great belching sound came from the exhaust, a huge cloud of black smoke rose up from behind *Quintana*'s stern, and the engine settled to a healthy, steady beat.

The sound was greeted by whoops and cries of "Well done, Dad" from inside the cabin.

"Great," yelled Andy. "Shake a leg, Sally. Let's get out of here."

They both leapt out of their bunks, instantly alert.

"You get the wheel, Sal. I'll go and deal with the anchor."

"Okay," Sally replied, scrambling up the steps and into the cockpit.

Andy grabbed the handle of the winch and started to haul the anchor in. Almost immediately it snagged on the coral below and jammed itself solid.

"Damn," said Andy. He eased off the chain and tried again. The same thing happened. "Sal."

"What?"

"Listen. The anchor's stuck. Can you just ease *Quintana* forward a little and see if we can free it?"

"Right." Sally pulled the throttle back so that the engine was just ticking over, then she nudged the clutch lever forward. *Quintana* lurched ever so slightly as the clutch engaged, then she began to inch forward very slowly.

"Take it steady," called Andy.

He kept up pressure on the winch handle, waiting for *Quintana*'s weight to free the chain. As soon as he felt it go slack, he wound in furiously. The anchor rose smoothly up from the seabed. "Well done,

Sal. We've got it. Now back her off, will you?"

"Okay." She pulled the lever back into reverse and *Quintana* lurched again very slightly and started to back up. Almost immediately Sally knocked her out of gear. Within a second or two *Quintana* was bobbing almost still again.

"Hold her there a second," Andy called, and jumped up onto the top of the doghouse. "There were quite a few rocks around here when we came in. Let's play safe."

He reached up and switched on the spotlight fastened to the main mast. He directed its powerful beam down over *Quintana*'s prow and into the sea, then jumped down again and went to the prow himself. He picked up the long pole and held it over the side. He probably wouldn't need it, but he wasn't taking any chances. Light beams trick the eyes and things underwater look farther away than they really are. He trusted Sally completely; they were all equally skilled at maneuvering *Quintana*. The pole was just an extra precaution.

"Right, Sal. She's all yours. Take her out. Real steady. I'll keep watch."

"Fine," Sally replied. "Here we go."

She swung the wheel to starboard and engaged gear again. The engine was thudding reassuringly now, and Sally increased the throttle very slightly. *Quintana*'s prow began to swing slowly around.

From the cockpit Sally could see the dense white cloud bank far in the distance, which almost permanently covered the high peaks of New Ireland. She swung the wheel back and straightened *Quintana* up, pointing her directly toward the clouds. The huge black bulk of South Daughter was now directly behind them.

Slowly and with infinite care, she began to ease *Quintana* away.

Andy kept careful watch and periodically called "Starboard" or "Port." Sally responded instantly and with calm efficiency, knowing that even at very slow speeds a scrape against viciously sharp coral can produce a lethal gash.

Eventually, when they were about two hundred yards out from the shore, Andy decided that they were in water deep enough to be safe and called back to her once more.

"Okay, Sal, that's it. Relax. We're out. Head her out to open sea."

Sally breathed a sigh of relief. "Thank goodness for that," she said. "Nerve racking, being near reefs."

She opened the throttle and *Quintana* began to surge forward. The familiar swish from her bow and the burble of the exhaust were welcome sounds.

Mom stuck her head out of the cabin. "I've plotted the course, more or less," she said. "I reckon if you go due west for about thirty minutes, then turn north-northwest, that'll put you in line with Kavieng."

Mom's course plotting was never very exact, but this time it didn't matter. There was a good moon and nothing in their way for at least a hundred miles.

"Your father says to forget the Duke of York Islands; they're too near Rabaul for comfort," added Mom. "Kavieng's the best part of two hundred miles so we should be safe there even if the volcano does blow."

"Due west it is," said Sally, and corrected *Quintana*'s course slightly. "Where is Dad, by the way?"

"Your father has gone to bed covered in

oil and stinking of diesel. He says you're in charge."

"That's fine with us," Sally replied. "You get some sleep now, too, Mom. We'll look after things up here."

"I will. I need a good night's sleep. Your father may be a little difficult tomorrow. He'll need pampering for a day or two."

She disappeared back down into the cabin.

"I'll leave you to it then, Sal," Andy said, as he stretched himself out on the roof of the doghouse. "You take the first shift. Wake me in about two hours and I'll take over. That way we'll both get some sleep."

"Right, I'll do that. There's a bit of cloud building up just out there to the northwest. We might get some rain later."

"Good," Andy replied. "It'll flatten the sea. We'll have a completely smooth trip right up to Kavieng. See you in two hours."

He placed his head on his arm and closed his eyes.

"See you. Good night."

"Good night."

Just before he drifted off to sleep, Andy's attention was caught by a faint sound.

Above the soft thud of the engine was another, deeper note. It sounded almost like a long, far-distant roll of thunder.

"A big storm on New Ireland," he decided.

But it seemed to go on too long to be thunder.

It was very faint and very far away, so he dismissed it and slept.

EIGHT

As soon as the first glimmers of dawn began to appear, Old Sea-bird reached out and grasped Kaleku's arm to wake him.

"Come," he said. "It is time to go."

Kaleku had been dreaming and he awoke afraid. In his dream he had been far out at sea, fishing. The morning was quiet and warm, and his canoe rose and fell gently on a soft swell. It was a lazy day, and the fish were reluctant to rise to his bait. His fishing line, weighted with a stone, snaked down into the depths and, now and then, he would give it a tug to attract a passing fish. Sometimes the line, wrapped around his hand, would jerk a little as something below explored the bait, but then it would go slack again as the fish lost interest and moved on.

Hours passed and the sun rose higher in the sky until, at noon, it was directly overhead, a fierce white disk pouring blinding light and heat down onto the surface of the sea. The sea became a searing mirror that hurt Kaleku's eyes. He sat with his head bowed and eyelids closed to avoid the pain.

Then the strangest of things happened.

With the curious illogicality of dreams, it started to go dark. It was as though great black storm clouds suddenly began to gather overhead.

But when Kaleku looked up he found that they were not storm clouds at all. Storm clouds billow and roll. They crash together in thunder, are shot through with lightning, and bring wind before them to churn the sea.

This was different.

Slowly, very slowly, a dense black curtain was drawn across the sky and dusk began to fall. At noon. Nothing else changed. The sea remained calm. The air remained warm.

It simply went dark.

Then, without any warning at all, without the preliminary nibblings that you always feel when a fish is preparing to take your bait, there was a violent wrench on the line, as though a huge fish swimming past at great speed had swallowed the bait and continued, without break, along its path.

Kaleku had no time to unwind the line from his hand. It dug deep and painfully into his flesh. He was torn from the canoe, dragged violently into the sea, and hauled, kicking and struggling, down into the depths.

Ahead of him, far down at the end of his line, he could see the shark that was pulling him. It was Lebigugu, the shark of the long head.

Desperately he tried to unravel the line from around his agonized hand, but it was so tight and so deeply embedded in his flesh that he could not move it. There was no escape. He would surely drown.

The hammerhead continued to arrow down until Kaleku could hold his breath no longer. His ears began to drum with pressure and his lungs felt as though they would burst. Terribly afraid, he knew that it was the end for him. He gave up the struggle to hold his breath and opened his lungs to let the water flood in.

And, again in the strangeness of a dream, he found that he could breathe.

Now he was nearing the ocean floor. The

deep sea landscape rose up toward him. The shark leveled out and slowed.

There was a strange green light everywhere. Pinnacles of jagged rock rose out of the white sand and loomed all around him. Long tentacles of seaweed reached up from the seabed.

Sharks were everywhere, sliding effortlessly in and out of the spires of rock, circling overhead, or resting, silhouetted dark against the silver sandbanks.

The line had gone slack, and Kaleku came to rest, standing, fearful, on the seafloor.

Then the real nightmare began.

As Kaleku watched, the sharks began to close in upon him. Those overhead continued to circle, but the circles became smaller and began to spiral down. Shadows broke away from the rocks and slowly turned to look at him, green light reflecting in their eyes and from their teeth.

The hammerhead had turned, too, and now hovered motionless, its great, ugly face leering with malice.

Slowly they all began to advance toward him.

The green light sparkled and flickered over their heads and bodies as they came, so that their shapes were indistinct, shimmering and shifting in the swirling currents.

And with a deep, unspeakable horror, Kaleku saw that they changed, transformed, as they came. At first only fleeting changes that vanished almost before they were seen, but that returned stronger, more recognizable, and more horrifying. Shark faces melted into faces almost human, and then back again. Fins momentarily became arms with searching fingers, then returned to fins. Long, oily bodies mutated before his eyes into grotesque caricatures of men.

Fishmen.

Mermen.

Gradually, as they neared, the strange, terrible transformations became complete.

Kaleku's mind screamed in horror.

Dropping down silently, one by one, the nightmare creatures began to surround him. Bathed in the unearthly green light, they were the color of rotting, putrefying flesh.

Dead men, drowned men, walking the ocean floor.

Kaleku could not move at all as, slowly, the ghastly circle began to close in upon him.

He could not even scream as the first bone white, rotting hand reached out and gripped his arm, a terrible, shark-toothed, human mouth opened in a hideous man-fish face, and a voice, distorted by the sea, said, "Come. It is time to go."

Of course it was only a dream.

But Kaleku woke up shaking with fear nevertheless. It had been so real.

"What is it?" asked Sea-bird. "Why do you shake?"

Kaleku was embarrassed. "Nothing, old man. It was nothing. Just a dream."

And that might have been all that was said at another time.

But this wasn't another time, it was now. And "now" was a special time. Shark Calling time. A time steeped in magic.

For Old Sea-bird, who knew the magic, there was no such thing as "just" a dream. Dream life was as much a reality as waking life. Dreams "happened." It was just that they took place somewhere else, in another world.

When Old Sea-bird hunted sharks through the nighttime oceans of his dreams, it didn't just take place in his head; he knew that. His spirit roamed the shark roads in the night, just as surely as his body had done in the day. Sleep, to Sea-bird, was the same as death. While your body sleeps your spirit is free to go where it will. When your body dies the spirit lives on, elsewhere.

The *masalai* were all around, if you knew where to look. The great shark hunters of the past lived on and hunted spirit sharks as they had done in life. Sometimes you almost saw them, shadows at the edges of your vision that vanished as you turned your head. But even if you couldn't see them, you knew they were there. For when you slept, and your spirit was freed, then you saw them.

Now, as Kaleku related his "dream," the old man was disturbed. The *masalai* were telling Kaleku something, but Sea-bird didn't know what it was.

The fishmen he could deal with. They

were only evil *masalai* sharks. There was magic for them.

But it was Lebigugu who had pulled Kaleku down, and that was puzzling. Of all the sharks in the ocean, the shark of the long head is the only one not hunted. His head is too big, and he is too tricky to snare. The hammerhead does not even come to the sound of the *larung*.

Yet Lebigugu's spirit had appeared to Kaleku.

And the sky had gone dark at noon.

What could it all mean?

The old man did not know. And there was nothing to be done now anyway. It was too late. Kaleku must go. The magic was done; the sharks waited.

But as he helped Kaleku prepare to leave, Sea-bird was worried. These were bad omens, he was sure of that. Things were wrong, out of joint. He would need to watch carefully. Read the sea.

Perhaps Kaleku would need him.

He betrayed none of his feelings to the boy.

"See," he said, as they walked down to

the canoe. Sea-bird had his many-pronged spear in his hand and was spearing at pebbles on the beach as they passed over them. "See. I spear the evil *masalai* sharks. This will fasten them to the bottom of the sea so they cannot rise."

"Yes," said Kaleku. He was irritated to hear that his voice sounded high pitched and nervous. He coughed as though he had needed to clear his throat.

It wasn't that he doubted Old Sea-bird's magic, but the dream remained with him, very vivid and very frightening. What he had to do was daunting enough and he hoped that the dream was not an omen of failure. He must try to put it out of his mind.

But out there, alone on the sea, it would be hard not to think of what might be lurking in the depths below. What if Sea-bird's magic didn't work after all? Men had gone out calling sharks and had not returned. So the magic wasn't infallible. Perhaps they, too, had dreamed as he had and had been dragged to the bottom of the sea by the *masalai.*

He shivered.

Sea-bird pretended not to notice.

They picked up the canoe between them and walked into the sea with it.

Sea-bird steadied it by holding the outrigger while Kaleku climbed in. It sank hardly at all into the water with Kaleku's added weight.

The old man grunted approvingly.

"It is a good canoe. You have done well."

And with only the traditional parting words, Kaleku began to paddle away.

When a Shark Caller sets out to sea no one, not even members of his family, comes to see him off, for leaving them may make him sad.

No one will wish him "Good luck" or "Good hunting," because he does not need good wishes. The magic will look after him.

When a Shark Caller's canoe is missing from the beach no one remarks on it or ever asks about him, because that might imply they were worried about him.

And when he returns with a shark tied to the sides of his canoe, no one congratulates him, because no one ever thought he would fail anyway.

So, strangely, on this great, momentous

occasion, when a young man sets out to face the greatest challenge of his life, there is no ceremony, no sense of occasion at all.

Only these simple words are spoken.

"Mi go nau."

And the reply.

"Orait. Yu go nau."

But though there may not be words, there are thoughts.

On this quiet morning, as Kaleku's paddle swished softly in the sea and the canoe pulled gently away from the shore, the young man was afraid.

And so, too, was Sea-bird.

NINE

༻༺

The night passed without event.

Mother and Father slept; Andy and Sally took two-hour shifts at the wheel and slept in between.

Dawn came and promised a sultry, humid day. The rain, which had been falling in the night, had cleared but had left the air heavy and water laden. As the sun crept higher in the sky and the heat began to threaten, a soft sea mist rose up toward New Ireland. The mist deadened sound, so that even *Quintana*'s throbbing engine seemed muffled.

When Andy took over the wheel just after eight o'clock, they were about sixty miles north of Rabaul, about the same from the nearest point of the New Ireland coast, and about 140 miles from their destination, Kavieng, at the northernmost tip of the island.

Sally had gone below and had climbed

into her bunk as soon as Andy had taken over from her.

Their parents were still sleeping.

Andy settled into the cockpit and checked the compass to satisfy himself that they were on course. Then he just sat, one hand on the wheel, content to feel *Quintana* sliding gently through the sea.

It was very calm, very quiet, and very relaxing.

Toward eight-thirty a slight following breeze sprang up. The mist lifted rapidly and New Ireland came into view, stretched along the horizon like a huge, basking whale. Behind *Quintana*, to the southwest, the cone of South Daughter was clearly visible.

Andy decided to hoist the mainsail. It would help the engine out a bit and might add a knot to their speed.

He fastened the wheel and let *Quintana* look after herself while he put the sail up. It took only a few minutes to winch it into place. It flapped a little halfheartedly at first but eventually filled. It wouldn't make much difference, but at least it was something.

That, then, is how things stood when it happened.

At 8:37 the technicians at the Rabaul Vulcanological Institute noticed that the seismograph needles had begun to thrash dementedly up and down on their graph papers.

In the next forty seconds a small part of the world's map changed.

During the night a huge pressure point had been building deep beneath the waters of Rabaul Harbor. Seething lava and immense clouds of gases had pushed the thin crust of the harbor floor upward until a huge, bulbous abscess had formed.

At 8:37 exactly, the abscess ruptured. Lava spilled out into the water and sulfurous gas rocketed up from the depths, screaming out through the surface of the sea in a great blast of heat.

In the first twenty seconds a crack two miles long and half a mile wide tore the seabed open.

And in the next twenty seconds a billion gallons of water began to drain into it. Roaring in tremendous torrents, it hurtled down the white-hot channels and fissures, screamed through passages and tunnels, deep into the molten heart of the earth. Instantly vaporizing, the water became huge clouds of pressurized, superheated steam that rolled and crashed with hurricane force throughout the bubbling lava fields.

Here and there the water tumbling onto the lava cooled it, so that it solidified and closed exits where the pressure might have escaped; so pressure built elsewhere as steam, mingled with one-thousand-degree-centigrade gases, roared through further channels, seeking escape.

At 8:37 and forty seconds the earth could stand no more. The miles of underground channels pulsated and heaved under the strain as the huge gas clouds forced their arteries to the breaking point.

At that precise moment the entire end of the island, fifty square miles of land, with all it contained, ripped itself apart.

Rabalankaia, long dormant, vanished first. Great cracks appeared briefly in its sides and it exploded into a million pieces.

Impacted lava, squeezed through a thousand underground passages, coursed through the ground and found release through South Daughter, who lurched and shuddered briefly as though a vast fist pushed her up from somewhere deep in the ground. Then she, too, blew herself apart, her body fragmented into a cloud of rock and earth, hurled miles into the air with the ease of a child throwing up a handful of pebbles.

Rabaul, sitting in the apex of the caldera, stood no chance. A gigantic hand seemed to grip the entire town and crumple it. Twenty thousand homes, the huge shipping wharf, and the oceangoing ships moored at it simply began to sink into the mountainside, sucked in by the heaving earth. Then it was all spat out again as a torrent of lava spewed up from the depths of the volcano. Whole houses, incandescent with heat, sailed through the air like meteors, terrible, unearthly shooting stars arcing across the sky and dropping, sizzling, into the waters of the harbor.

For miles inland nothing survived. A great *nuee ardente,* a murderous blast of sulfurous gas and white-hot particles, tore out of the side of shattered Matupi and cut a swath of fiery devastation two miles wide across the land. Whole villages were incinerated, the people in them instantaneously carbonized. One second they were there; the next, all that remained of them was smoldering ash.

And, finally, ruined Matupi, writhing in its death throes, gave out its last cry.

With a great, unearthly roar the volcano vomited a gigantic gush of ash, stone fragments, and molten rock vertically, ten miles into the air.

A huge column of fire and smoke rocketed skyward into the atmosphere, where it began to spread and obliterate the sun.

The final release had been found.

Forty seconds and the world was forever changed.

The Gazelle Peninsula, with its hundred villages, its schools, its hospitals, its plantations and forests, was gone.

Rabaul was gone.

And in numbers no one would ever be able to count, the people were gone.

All gone.

In forty seconds.

———

Glancing back over *Quintana*'s stern, Andy could see the perfect volcanic cone of South Daughter, the only part of the Gazelle coastline still visible, silhouetted between sea and sky.

Then, without warning, it disappeared and its place was taken by a cloud of black smoke.

At first he couldn't believe it. He blinked rapidly, thinking his eyes were playing tricks.

It was the absence of sound that fooled him, that made it all seem unreal. But sound travels more slowly.

The sound came a few seconds later. A long, muffled crack shuddered out across the sea, a distant, unearthly roll of thunder in a cloudless tropical sky.

The sound froze him. This was it. It had happened. They had gotten out just in time.

He knocked the engine out of gear.

"Hey," he called down into the cabin. "Quick! Get up! Mom, Dad, Sally, come and see. The volcano's gone up. It's just blown itself out. I saw it."

There was a scrabbling and muttering from below, and the family, bleary eyed but instantly awake, emerged into the cockpit.

"It's South Daughter," Andy said. "I just happened to be looking at it. It just vanished."

"Oh," said Peter Thompson. "That's a surprise. South Daughter's been dormant for centuries. It was Matupi they were expecting to blow."

"Well," added Ann Thompson hopefully, "it doesn't look too bad. It's blown out this side, away from Rabaul. Let's hope it stops there."

But, of course, it didn't.

The next second a vast column of fire and smoke hurtled up into the sky.

And when the next sound came, they knew that Rabaul was finished.

Whatever made that sound was pure, malignant devastation.

It was more a force than a sound. It was visual sound; they saw it shake the sky. A great, battering wave of sound.

Nothing back there could have survived.

"Dear God," said Peter Thompson.

"Oh," gasped Sally. Her hand had flown to her mouth in shock. "Oh, the poor people. I hope they got out."

"They might have." Ann Thompson's voice quavered a little with shock. "The volcano people were watching carefully. They probably sounded the alarm last night, but we couldn't hear it."

"Yes," said Peter Thompson. "Everything was in hand. Their evacuation plans were excellent, I know that. They'll have gotten everybody out."

"Do you think we should go back? See if we can help?" asked Andy.

"No. No point. The navy is on standby if anything else happens, and the army has camps set up in the Baining hills for the evacuees. There would be nothing at all we could do. We'd just be in the way."

"Okay," replied Andy. "At least we're safe. Thank goodness we got out when we did. Twelve hours earlier we'd have been sitting right by South Daughter."

"I know. Don't think about it."

"Look," said Sally. "The column of smoke. It's spreading out into a mushroom cloud, just like an atom bomb."

"Yes, so it is. Though I should think the explosion there was more like a hundred atom bombs."

"Come on," said Dad. "Let's get away from here. That cloud will spread over us before long. We'll be covered in hot ash. Give it two or three hours and it will be over us. Let's see if we can stay ahead of it."

"Right," said Andy.

But for a while no one moved. The dull, distant roar and the terrible pictures they were painting in their minds held them transfixed.

Finally they turned away and prepared to move on.

Andy engaged the engine and the big brass propeller started to turn. Sally sat down beside him in the cockpit, silent and white faced. Peter and Ann Thompson went below.

Within minutes *Quintana* was back up to five knots again, heading away, its occupants inwardly torn between sorrow for the people of Rabaul and thankfulness that they themselves had escaped the danger.

But there was another danger that they couldn't see. Something they couldn't know.

The devastation in Rabaul Harbor had been so cataclysmic that its ramifications were not yet over. The huge movements of the earth, the shiftings and foldings of molten rock, the pressures of steam and gases, all had set up a deep undersea current that was swirling and sliding across the shattered end of the island. Its origins were deep in the ocean, but great rippling shock waves were rising up. Shock waves so huge that they would roll the sea's surface over onto itself and send it hurtling down the 120-mile-wide channel between New Britain and New Ireland in a *tsunami* a hundred feet high.

Tsunami.

Tidal wave.

TEN

۞

Andy watched the column of smoke and ash anxiously as he guided *Quintana* along. The tremendous heat pouring into the air could bring storms later.

With luck *Quintana* would be safely moored in Kavieng Harbor by then.

Reason told him that they could probably stay ahead of the ash. The force was blasting it hundreds of miles into the sky, into space even, so it would be a long time yet before it started to fall to earth. And when it did, its long journey would have cooled it. It would be a nuisance rather than a danger.

So, he kept telling himself, there was no need for fear.

Instinct, however, was telling him another story.

At first he couldn't put his finger on

what was wrong. It just seemed that things felt different.

Of course things were very different. There had been a great disaster. But it was far away and so unreal as to be beyond imagination.

Things here, on *Quintana*, in this small part of the ocean, hadn't really changed. The engine still throbbed reassuringly; *Quintana*'s prow whispered through the swells; cups and plates rattled in the galley; the sun still shone down from a clear sky.

Things were normal.

Except that for Andy they weren't.

The feel of everything, the "atmosphere" of the place, was changed.

Nothing seemed to be quite right. The voices and noises from below seemed vaguely muffled and flat, like voices in a snow-covered landscape. *Quintana*'s motion seemed different: a change so slight that Andy dismissed it as imagination. But it troubled him even when he had dismissed it. She felt to be riding the swells a little less surely, as though she were being pulled ever so slightly back in her progress. He looked over the stern to see if anything had snagged on the propeller and was holding her back, but there was nothing. He looked out ahead at the surface of the sea and there was nothing to account for it there, either.

Andy furrowed his brow with worry. He wondered briefly whether to call his father up from below and tell him what he felt. But what would he tell him? That he had a "funny feeling" about the sea? He could imagine what his father would say about that.

So he did nothing except keep *Quintana* heading for the safety of Kavieng. He settled back down at the wheel and tried to put the disturbing thoughts out of his mind. Provided the engine didn't give up on them, there was nothing to worry about. By nightfall they would be approaching New Ireland, and tomorrow they could negotiate the tortuous channels into Kavieng Harbor. He pushed the engine up carefully to full throttle, listening for any signs of complaint. When none came he relaxed a little as the ship picked up speed. Whatever happened, *Quintana* would see them through. She always had.

About half a mile ahead he noticed a

huge flock of birds swirling over the sea's surface, hundreds of ragged specks plunging into the sea and rising again. He picked up the binoculars and focused on the birds. There were thousands, not hundreds, and they were feeding on a huge shoal of fish bubbling on the surface of the sea. The sunlight flickered on the fishes' scales so that the sea itself seemed molten silver. Andy had to screw up his eyes against the glare. As he watched, a dark, triangular fin slid silently into his vision.

Andy caught his breath. Although the shark was half a mile away, the binoculars gave the fin a shocking proximity, enough to send a shudder of fear through him.

He kept the binoculars fixed on the fin as it cut effortlessly through the blinding water, a black, razor-sharp knife slicing through satin. Then, ahead of the fin, a great, ugly head rose through the sea's surface and with careless, disdainful ease plucked one of the birds from the air.

The shark was joined by another and another.

Andy adjusted the binoculars so that he had a greater field of vision. It was hard to tell how many sharks there were. They moved so quickly, sliding in and out of each other or surfacing and diving, that it was impossible to count them. Andy guessed there were about twenty.

The attack was so sudden that many of the birds were taken by surprise, swallowed before they knew what was happening. But within seconds it was all over. The huge flock scattered, exploded away from the fish shoal, whirled briefly in a panicked moment of indecision, then congealed into a single mass and spiraled away.

Andy watched them spinning upward, dark against the sky, then let the binoculars descend again to the sea.

The terrible fins still wove their patterns through the water, but more quickly now, jerky and frantic. The pack had gone into a feeding frenzy and were simply hurling themselves through the fish shoal, mindlessly gorging themselves.

The surface of the sea was no longer silver.

It was red.

Andy put the glasses down. He had seen enough.

Nobody blamed Andy for what happened next. Nobody would have dreamed of blaming him.

But he blamed himself. He should have told his father that things didn't seem right. Perhaps nothing could have been done anyway. Who could have put those few vague clues together and come up with an answer even remotely like what happened?

More importantly, he shouldn't have been watching the sharks feeding. If he'd been concentrating on *Quintana,* he might have realized sooner that something was happening. What he would have done if he had realized, he had no idea. But he might have been able to do something. Even if he had only been able to get the sail down, it might have helped.

As he laid the binoculars down, he became aware of a change in the background sound of the day. The engine was throbbing steadily, just as before, the exhaust rumbling softly in the water behind him. Far off, the volcano still roared, a dull, distant thunder.

But above these things he heard a hissing, an insistent sibilance like a vent of escaping steam. He cocked his head to one side, trying to establish from where it came. The sound increased slightly in volume. He looked out over the sea to port and starboard. He began to feel uneasy. The sea was still calm and there was nothing in sight.

The noise began to grow, the hiss deepening to a long, susurrating roar. It seemed almost to come from above him. He tipped his head backward and looked up. The sky was clear and cloudless, with no sign of turbulence at all.

The sound increased inexorably, not loud yet but of great power. It sounded like water, like the hiss of a great cataract rushing to the edge of a precipice.

Andy felt the hair on the back of his neck begin to rise.

Quintana rode to the top of a swell and paused. Once again Andy felt that she was being held back.

The roar increased, deepened.

It was coming from behind *Quintana.*

The noise was behind them!

Andy spun around.

Hurtling toward them, blotting out the horizon, stretching as far as he could see in each direction, was an immense, curling wave. A hundred feet high, 150, it was impossible to tell.

For a moment he was paralyzed by disbelief.

Nothing, no ship on earth, could ride a wave like that.

"Dad," he screamed. "Get up here quick!"

The urgency of his voice brought his father out into the cockpit immediately.

"What? What is it?"

"Look behind. Tidal wave. What do we do?"

"Dear God, where did that come from? Quick, Andy, get up front and close the for'ard hatch. Ann, Sally, get in your bunks. *Now!* Don't ask why. Just get in and pad yourselves with pillows and things."

Andy ran forward and battened down the hatch. His hands shook as he spun the clasps down, but he had it done in seconds. He turned and looked again at the wave. There was no telling at what speed it was approaching, but it was coming very fast indeed. They had very little time before it would hit.

"Get back here fast. Get down below with your mother and sister." Peter Thompson had clipped on his safety belt and fastened the line to the cockpit rail.

Andy hesitated.

"Come on. Move it. Get below. Then I can shut you all in."

Andy closed the doghouse hatch and fastened the double doors leading into the cabin. "I'll stay up here with you, Dad. You might need some help."

"Like blazes you will. Get below when you're told."

"I'm staying."

Peter Thompson looked hard at his son, then gave up the battle. "All right. Get your line on."

Andy slipped into his safety harness and clipped his line to the rail.

"Now," said Peter Thompson. "Let's see what we can do."

He grabbed the wheel and they both turned and watched the wave approach.

The last seconds were the most terrifying of all. The sea around them started to swirl and move, agitated by the pressure of the huge wall of water pushing toward them.

The sound of the wave became deafening as it neared. *Quintana* began to be pushed forward, her stern lifting as the first outriders of the huge moving mass hit.

Her stern continued to lift as she gathered speed.

In the end neither father nor son had any idea what to do. There was nothing that could be done, except hang on and hope.

Peter Thompson clung desperately to the wheel.

Andy grasped the rail and prayed.

Quintana's stern rose until the ship was standing almost vertical, nose down, caught in the vortex of the wave.

With a desperate, nightmare slowness, she began to tip forward.

The last thing Andy remembered was the sickening thump as *Quintana* toppled, head over heels, and crashed heavily into the trough at the base of the great wave.

Then there was only blackness.

ELEVEN

&

Gradually, as he fell into a steady rhythm, Kaleku's nerves began to calm. Now and then, in the first half hour or so, he looked back, gaining reassurance from the sight of land and the solitary figure of Sea-bird standing motionless on the beach watching him depart. He convinced himself that Sea-bird would watch over him, would know if he got into danger, and would help. Sea-bird had much powerful magic if it was needed.

The figure became smaller and smaller, until all Kaleku could see was the bright red of the old man's *lap-lap*, vivid against the dull green of the island's vegetation. Then Kaleku consigned himself to the sea ahead and turned no more.

He was pleased with his canoe. It slid lightly and easily through the waves at each pull of the paddle. Before long he began to feel that it was a part of him, as easy to move and control as his arms and legs.

The dream began to let go its grip on his mind as the familiarity of the ocean surrounded him. This was the sea he knew. The sun beating down on him began to drive away the fears of the night. He felt strong and took pleasure in his strength, enjoying the ease with which his muscles took the strain as he drove the paddle deep into the water and pulled hard away from the shore.

The day seemed right. The sea was calm and friendly. He was well equipped and well prepared. He knew what he had to do. The magic had been made. Now it was up to him.

Only one thing marred his mood, nagged painfully at the back of his mind. He wished that he had told Sea-bird about it but had been embarrassed to do so. Perhaps Sea-bird would have had magic for that, too. Or perhaps he would have been angry at Kaleku's carelessness. But it was too late now. If the blood on the stone shark's teeth was an omen, then there was nothing to be done.

In a way he wasn't frightened by omens anyway. Although the society in which he had grown up was ruled by magic and superstition it wasn't necessary to believe everything. You *couldn't* believe everything. Your eyes told you not to believe.

Sometimes the rainmaker failed to make rain. He would bluster and stand on his dignity when people complained. He would blame his failure on strong, evil *masalai* who were blocking his magic. But people were not fooled.

Perhaps even Old Sea-bird's magic couldn't control everything.

For the moment only one thing mattered. *Find the shark roads and begin.* Then time would tell.

So he simply paddled and tried to put all thoughts out of his mind, except the sea ahead of him. Now and then he would break his progress to glance over his shoulder. The coast of New Ireland, of home, gradually dwindled to a faint pencil line of blue, then eventually vanished altogether.

Briefly he felt a shock of isolation when he turned and saw that the land had finally gone. He paused and looked ahead, his newly found confidence momentarily shaken once more. The sea looked grayer, more threatening.

He let the canoe ride gently on the swells. In the oppressive silence he was suddenly acutely aware of his vulnerability. And at that moment, in the strange way that the mind has of playing tricks, a vivid picture scorched across his brain. For a split second he saw the huge hammerhead shark of his dreams circling far below him, its great gray bulk slipping silently and effortlessly through the ocean shadows.

He found that his hands were trembling, and he gripped the paddle shaft tightly to steady them. His knuckles whitened with the strain.

Then he grunted with annoyance at his cowardice, instantly ashamed that these thoughts had come into his head. He was behaving like a frightened child, allowing monsters of his imagination to invade him. Nothing had changed. The sea around him was the same as before. He was no more alone, no more in danger than when land was in sight. It was still there, just beyond the horizon.

He took a deep breath and pushed his fear down, quelling the instinct to swing his canoe around and paddle hard back to safety. Such a thing was unthinkable anyway. He could not return, he knew that. Whatever was in store for him, he had to face it. To return without a shark would bring unbearable shame, would prove that he was indeed a frightened child.

Gradually his hands steadied and his heart stopped thumping. He took control of himself once more.

You're thinking too much, he told himself. *Concentrate on what is happening, not on what might happen. Deal with things as they arise.*

He lifted his paddle, plunged it deep into the water, and began to move again. He fixed his mind on his movements and nothing else, willing each action of his body to take place.

Lift your arms. Forward with the paddle. Into the water. Pull.

And so he progressed, mind calmed by repetition, fears pushed aside by steady concentration on the job at hand.

Soon he felt better again and smiled wryly at himself, ashamed at his behavior and thankful that there had been nobody around to see his fear. He began to relax once more.

It couldn't be too difficult, after all. Men from his village had hunted sharks since time began. Hardly anyone ever failed. Why should he be different? He was young and strong and quick witted. Sea-bird's magic was there in the canoe with him. What did he have to fear?

So get on with it, he told himself. *Find the shark roads and get it over with. And stop letting your imagination run away with you.*

He glanced up at the position of the sun. It was well up in the sky now, and he guessed that he had been traveling for about two hours. By noon he would be well out into the channel between New Ireland and New Britain, where the shark roads were plentiful.

He increased the power of his paddle strokes, surging the canoe along with regained confidence and determination.

He was in charge again. His imagination was under control.

But what happened next was not imagination.

His guess that he had been traveling for two hours was very nearly right.

Very nearly.

The time was now 8:37.

TWELVE

§

Kaleku's confidence was short-lived. The explosion from over the sea shattered it.

He stopped paddling and watched as the column of black smoke climbed into the sky. His heart sank.

The spirits were battling, and he was caught up in it.

He remembered the slight shaking of the earth as he had sat on the beach. That had been the beginning, the first rumblings, but he had not known it.

The dream began to make sense. Already the sky was darkening to the southwest. The dream was a prophecy after all. Not that it made much difference. There was no turning back.

Perhaps at that moment, secretly in his heart, Kaleku knew that he would never return from the sea. But he simply turned and resumed his paddling.

Minutes later he began to feel the first, small differences in the sea. A faint pulling motion seemed to suck his canoe back from the crests of the swells. He looked back to the south. The sealine at the horizon was unchanged.

He put his paddle down in the bottom of the canoe and stood, staring hard, trying to read what it was that he felt was wrong.

And as he watched, the horizon began to transform. The line was no longer flat. It shimmered and moved, undulated.

Tsunami.

A *tsunami* was building.

Quickly he set about preparing for it.

He looked hard at the rope lashings fastening the outrigger and remembered how irritated he had felt with Sea-bird when the old man had fussed and complained at their earlier inadequacy. Now he was glad. The canoe was strong and firm. He pulled out the coils of bush rope from the prow of the canoe. With one piece he bundled together the rattle, club, and spear. He placed them all in the bottom of the canoe and lashed them firmly to his seat. Then he cut a short length of rope, tied one end to the shaft of his paddle and the other to his wrist. Everything was now secured.

He undid the longer coil of rope and pushed an end through one of the holes where the outrigger spars were fastened to the hull. He tied this securely. The other end of the rope he tied around his waist. The greatest danger of all was that he would become separated from his canoe and never find it again. Now he would remain attached to it, whatever happened.

He stood again and scanned the sea around him. It was still calm, but heavy with expectation. The swells had flattened, pulled back in preparation.

The horizon was boiling now. Long fingers of white water shot up into the sky. Far away to the southwest, briefly silhouetted against the blackness of the roaring smoke, he could see a tiny patch of white. He narrowed his eyes to focus it, but it remained indistinct. He decided it was probably a sail, perhaps one of the big *motu* sailing canoes from New Britain. He hoped its occupants were well prepared.

Gradually the horizon rose and rose, and he started to hear the menacing hiss of the wave. Through the soles of his feet he could feel the canoe beginning to tremble as the building *tsunami* pushed shock waves before it.

The tremble rose up through his body and settled in his heart. The horizon was still rising and he realized with a shock that coursed through his body, that this was no ordinary *tsunami*. This was going to be no twenty-foot or thirty-foot wave such as he had experienced before. This was going to be much, much bigger.

He found that he could not take his eyes off the southern horizon. The wave was beginning to take form, to come into focus. Gradually it resolved itself.

This was not a wave. This was a mountain of water, a vast gray wall surging toward him.

The canoe began to rock, gently at first, but with increasing violence as the shock waves hit.

Kaleku sat again, plunged his paddle into the sea, and pulled the canoe around so that it was backed onto the approaching wave.

Then he began to paddle away from it, pulling with all his strength.

He had no thought of escaping the wave. That was impossible. But if he was moving ahead of it, he might just be able to minimize its effect, perhaps be able to ride with it, to rise up with it, so its terrible power did not hit him with such force.

The sea was in turmoil now. One moment the canoe was forced up to the top of a shock wave, the next plunged, with a sickening crash, into a deep trough. Behind him he could hear the hiss rising to a scream.

It was almost upon him.

His mind was now as perturbed as the sea. His dream returned with numbing clarity. He saw himself once again carried down into the depths, and the horrific faces of the phantom fishmen appeared, leering and mocking, in his brain.

Nothing could survive the power of this. The entire ocean was on the move. His canoe would be shattered. He would be shattered.

This was the end. He had failed before he had even started.

In the last seconds he felt the great wall

of water begin to loom over him. The canoe began to lift as though pushed up by a huge, violent hand rising out of the seabed.

Then there was only blackness.

THIRTEEN

ε³

In the first terrible seconds of rising from unconsciousness, he registered two things.

He was in the water.

Something in the water was brushing against him.

He found himself screaming. He lashed out in panic, flailing his arms and legs with the strength of horror.

"No-o-o-o-o," he screamed. "Get away. Get away."

Then his violent thrashing took him under the surface, and he choked as bitter, acrid seawater rushed into his stomach and lungs. He came up again, gasping and retching with nausea. His throat burned as though he had swallowed acid, and he was blinded by the stinging salt water.

But still he kicked out with his legs and beat the surface of the sea with his hands. His writhings took him down again, but he was sufficiently in control of himself to close his mouth before he went under.

The thing brushed against his skin again, but this time it encircled his body and pinned his arms to his sides. He struggled, trying to throw off the powerful grip, but it was viselike, immovable.

Yet, though he was pinioned, panic still drove him to extremities of strength. He lurched his body from side to side and continued to lunge out into the water with his legs, hoping at least to land a blow that would deter the creature, however briefly.

He surfaced again, still trapped in the powerful, terrible embrace, but still trying desperately to break free.

It was only then that he heard the shouting. His ears were filled with water, so the sound seemed to come from far away.

"Stop!" the voice called. "Andy. Andy. It's me. For God's sake, stop it."

He stilled his panicked movements momentarily, to listen.

"It's me. Dad. Calm yourself. Are you trying to kill me or what?"

The grip on his arms released, and Andy raised his hands up to his face to rub his blind eyes. His father's hand gripped him just above the elbow and supported him in the water.

"Now keep still. The lifelines are trapped under the keel and all tangled up. We'll get those off first."

Slowly more things began to register in Andy's mind.

Behind his father's voice was another voice.

"Help," the voice called. "Help me. Oh please, help me."

Andy thought he knew the voice but, strangely, he couldn't quite place it. He puzzled over it, listening intently.

"Help," it called, hoarse with fear. "Help."

It was very muffled. He shook his head hard to try to clear his ears of water. It didn't work. Everything felt fuzzy. He pinched his nose hard and blew.

That worked. His ears popped and he could hear again.

Then, quite suddenly, he was aware of pain.

Every slight movement as he trod water caused him agony. He gasped and shouted out as he felt his father fumbling with the catch of the safety harness at his waist. It felt as though the harness were cutting him in half, a fiery pressure around his middle that restricted his breathing to tiny, shallow gulps of air.

And still the strangely familiar voice was calling out. "Help. Help me."

Part of him knew that he should be doing something about it, but he was incapable of doing anything except keeping himself afloat. He felt as though he were in a dream from which he knew he must wake up. Things were happening around him, but he seemed disconnected from them, withdrawn into himself and his own pain.

His eyes began to clear, and he became aware of the sunlight dazzling him on the surface of the water. He rubbed them hard again and they cleared more.

The voice calling for help continued, and it began to worry him now. He shook his head, wondering what he could do.

His father surfaced beside him and came into his vision, blurred but recognizable.

"Right, you're free of your harness.

Quick, get back on board and see to Mom and Sally. I'm still tangled up."

"Yes. Yes, of course."

Andy heard himself say the words, but he still seemed disembodied, as though, floating in the sea, he was floating in space, looking down on himself and hearing himself speak. He still made no move, did not know what move to make, and continued to tread water confusedly. He looked at his father wonderingly.

Then, suddenly, Peter Thompson did something so shocking, so completely out of character, that Andy could not believe it had happened.

He drew back his arm and hit Andy hard across the face.

Andy gasped with pain, a deep exhalation of shock and outrage. Anger flashed across his eyes.

His father had hit him. Why? Never in his life had his father hit him.

What in heaven's name did he think he was doing?

But at the moment that his hand shot up to his cheek, reality surged back into

Andy's mind. Lost in the strange limbo world of deep shock, he had been unable to deal with the situation, a danger to himself and useless to others who needed him. The slap had brought him out of it.

"Sorry," said his father. "I had to do something. Now, quickly, pull yourself together. *Quintana*'s still afloat, just. I'm still tangled up with this line. Get on board now. They need help. I'll be with you as soon as I can."

Now, at last, Andy began to resolve the picture.

He found himself floating about ten feet from *Quintana*. She lay low in the water, with only an inch or so of her hull showing. The masts were gone.

And that was all Andy had time to take in before he started swimming. Sally was still calling out, her voice filled with panic and distress.

"Help me. I can't move. Please help me."

"Sal. Sally. Hang on. I'm coming."

Sally heard him. "Andy. Oh, Andy. Quickly. I'm trapped. Quickly."

He struck out hard and within seconds was alongside *Quintana*'s stern. She was so

low in the water that her deck seemed almost level with the surface.

He took hold of the buckled stern rail,
heaved himself quickly on board, and stood.

"Sal. Where are you?"

"We're in the forward cabin. Quick,
Andy. The water's almost up to the roof.
I'm holding Mom up. She's unconscious.
Quick."

"Hold on. I'm coming."

He ran quickly along the deck and took
hold of the cabin hatch. He pulled hard but
it was locked from the inside. He abandoned
it, rushed back, and jumped down into the
cockpit. The cockpit well was entirely full of
water. The doghouse was completely gone,
torn away by the impact of the capsize, and
the great, jagged hole in the deck revealed
the galley was full of water, too.

He plunged straight down the galley
steps and found that the water here was
right up to the roof. Taking a deep breath,
he submerged and kicked himself off from
the steps, swimming hard toward the forward cabin door. He banged heavily against
it, grabbed the handle, and pulled.

Nothing happened.

He shifted his position, floating a little to one side. Then he lay on his back, put one foot against the door frame, and pulled again. And again nothing happened. The door was jammed tight. He gave another huge heave.

Come on, he shouted in panic in his mind. *Come on. Move.*

But he failed again.

That was the limit of his breath. His lungs were throbbing with pain, so he turned quickly in the water, set his feet firmly against the door, and pushed himself back through the galley.

He surfaced into the flooded cockpit again and shouted to Sally.

"Sally. Hold on a little longer. The door's stuck. I'm just getting my breath. I'm coming straight back."

He glanced out to where his father was still struggling to disentangle himself from the web of rigging. His face was contorted with effort. Or pain.

"You all right, Dad?"

"I'm all right. Nearly free, I think. Ignore me. I'll be with you in a second or two. See to your mother and Sally. For God's sake, hurry."

Andy took another deep breath and plunged down into the galley again.

Be cool, he told himself. *Panic kills.*

This time, instead of simply grabbing the door and pulling, he swam forward to examine it closely. He couldn't see very clearly, as his own shadow was blocking the light, but he ran his hands down the door frame on each side and quickly located what was blocking it. The stove had been wrenched from its fixings and lay on the floor, wedged between the door and the adjacent cupboards. He sank down to his knees, took hold of it, and yanked it out of the way.

The door opened easily. He kicked with his feet and swam through.

Here the cabin roof sloped gradually upward, following the line of *Quintana*'s sheer. And it was this small difference, this chance freak of *Quintana*'s design, that had saved them. Without it they both would surely have drowned. The slope of the deck meant that there was a gap between the water's surface and the cabin roof. At the galley door end it was no more than an inch, but at the forward end the gap had increased to about six inches. It was here that Andy found his mother and Sally.

As he swam forward underwater he could see his mother's body floating upright, her dress billowing out around her. Sally's arm was around her neck, supporting her. Panic started to rise again.

He surfaced into the air gap and found that there was just sufficient room to breathe if he tilted his head back.

Sally was whimpering with fear now, her face twisted in distress.

"Oh, Andy. Quickly. Take hold of Mom and keep her head up. My legs are trapped and I couldn't let go of her to free them. They hurt terribly. If *Quintana* goes any lower we'll drown."

She spoke rapidly and disjointedly. She was close to hysteria.

Andy took hold of her arm to steady her.

"It's all right. I'll have you out of here soon."

He tried to put his feet on the cabin floor so that he could support his mother but sank down too far. The floorboards were gone and he found himself descending into the bilges. He kicked up again, took hold of the rail around the top bunk, and held on tightly to that. With his other arm he encircled his mother's body and took her weight.

"Right, I've got her, Sal. See if you can free yourself."

Sally released her arm from around her mother's neck, slipped her head under the water, and started to wriggle her upper body forward so she could reach her legs. She struggled for perhaps half a minute, then lurched back again into her original position and surfaced into the air, gasping.

"There's something jammed in the end of the bunk right across my shins. I can't move it."

"Right. Don't panic. Keep your head up and take deep breaths. You support Mom again and I'll see what it is."

Sally put her arm around her mother's neck and Andy released his hold. He pulled himself down to the end of the bunk. The air gap was too little here to be of any use, so he submerged. He found that it was getting increasingly difficult for him to see underwater. His eyes seemed not to focus properly. He became aware of the pungent taste of diesel fuel in his mouth. He could see Sally's legs as far down as her knees, but then they disappeared. A jagged piece of planking was wedged between the bunk and the cabin roof, pinning Sally into her bunk.

His breath started to run out so he pulled himself back to the other end and surfaced beside Sally's face. His eyes were stinging now, and he wondered briefly whether the diesel would make him blind.

At that moment there was a banging from the deck above and his father's voice bellowed down.

"Andy. Unlock the hatch. I can't shift it."

The hatch. Why hadn't he thought to open it? It would at least have given some light.

He reached up and turned the wheel of the lock. The cover was instantly wrenched off from above and Peter Thompson's head and shoulders appeared in the opening.

The light flooding into the cabin hurt Andy's eyes even more, but even with his distorted vision he could see that blood was streaming down his father's face from a deep gash in his forehead, and his left shoulder seemed to be touching his ear.

"Dad. Listen. Sally's trapped. I'm trying to free her. See if you can get Mom out."

"Yes."

His father leaned down into the cabin and circled his right arm under her armpits.

"I can't lift her out. My shoulder's broken again. I'll support her. Get Sally free."

Sally was crying now, sobbing with fear. Andy reached out and touched her face.

"Just another minute. I know what's holding you in. Just hang on."

"Keep calm," her father added. "We're not sinking. Andy'll have you out in a second."

Andy took another deep breath and sank down again. This time he closed his eyes to protect them and felt his way along the bunk. His hands arrived at the planking and he briefly explored around it until he could feel Sally's legs. The wood was biting deeply into her flesh and her legs felt very cold to his touch. The wood was at an angle, wedged firmly, and he judged that he would do the least damage to Sally's legs if he knocked it downward, with the angle, rather than trying to pull it out from the bunk. Briefly he opened his eyes again, took aim at the top of the plank where it was jammed against the bunk roof, and hit it hard with the side of his fist.

It moved half an inch but did not come away.

Even under the water he heard Sally scream with pain.

His stomach turned over at the thought of the agony he must have caused her. But there was nothing else he could do.

He smashed at it again with all his strength. Pain shot up his arm from the impact, but this time the plank released and floated up to rest against the roof. Sally was free. He grabbed her by the waistband of her shorts, hauled her out of the bunk, and pushed her upward, toward the hatch. He trod water, supporting her until she had her arms out of the hatch, then planted both his feet firmly on the edge of the bottom bunk, put his shoulder under her bottom, and hoisted her up so she could squeeze past her mother's limp body and out onto the deck.

"Now, Dad, let's get Mom out. You haul and I'll push."

He sank down in the water again and grasped his mother around the knees. Then, with his feet again on the bunk, he heaved her upward, too. She was a dead weight, inert, but together they managed to get her out through the hatch so that she was sitting on the side, her legs still dangling down in the water. From there, his father and Sally dragged her out and laid her on the deck.

Andy followed, pulling himself up onto the deck, where he collapsed, face down, gasping and choking with the effort and the foul-tasting water. When he opened his eyes he found that everything was misted and contorted. He prayed silently that his sight was not permanently damaged, but he said nothing. He could see well enough to know that Sally was sitting against a buckled rail post, crying uncontrollably and holding her legs. Rivers of blood ran down them and stained the deck a shocking scarlet.

"Andy, get over here quick! Help me get your mother onto her feet. I can't do it with one arm."

Andy pushed himself up on to his knees and then stood.

"What for? What are you doing?"

"We've got to get the water out of her. Quickly, get behind her."

Andy grasped her under her arms and together they hauled her upright.

"Now, let her bend forward."

"Right."

Andy slid his arms down to her waist and let the top half of her body fold over his arms. Her weight nearly pulled him off his feet. He staggered slightly, then regained balance.

"Now squeeze. Hard."

He pulled her back against himself with as much force as he could summon. A gush of water shot out of her mouth and splashed onto the deck. Immediately she began to gasp and cough and retch.

"Well done, boy. Well done. Now let's lower her down."

Awkwardly they managed to slide her down onto the deck. She was coughing alarmingly and water was still shooting from her mouth. But color was already beginning to return to her face.

"Good. Now put her in recovery position. She'll be all right in a few minutes."

Andy raised her arms over her head and

rolled her over onto her face. Then he gently bent one arm and put it under her head and crooked one of her legs so her knee supported some of her body weight on the deck.

She began to splutter incoherently. She was trying to talk but the words would not come.

Peter Thompson placed his hand gently on his wife's brow and put his face down close to her ear.

"It's all right, love. Lie quiet. Everyone's all right. We're all alive. We're all here."

She nodded and made a weak effort at a smile. Her first thought, as always, had been for others, and Peter Thompson had known that. He stroked her hair gently to reassure her.

"Just take your time. Lie there until you feel better."

He looked at Sally.

"How about you? Report! Any injuries?" He snapped the words rather than spoke them.

Sally stopped crying and looked at her father. How could he be so brusque with her? She felt suddenly very angry that he should be so unsympathetic.

"Nothing I can't deal with," she snapped back, sulkily nursing her bleeding legs. By then she had examined them enough to know that they were only badly skinned. Nothing was broken.

Andy felt sorry for Sal, but she would realize later what her father was doing. The harshness of his tone was as effective as the slap he had given Andy.

Dad was just, in his efficient, clinical way, bringing everybody under control.

"Andy. Report!"

"Give me time, for goodness' sake. I haven't had time to think yet."

"We haven't got time. *Quintana* is swamped. Report!"

Andy examined himself.

"Nothing serious. My head hurts like hell. And I can't believe my bottom half is still attached to my top. Otherwise I'm fine."

He lifted his T-shirt. There was a livid red-blue welt around his stomach where his safety harness had bitten into him. But it was only bruised, it wasn't bleeding.

"What about you, Dad?" asked Sally. She looked a little shamefaced now, realizing that she had been thinking only of herself a moment ago.

"Bruises only, I think. Except my flaming collarbone's gone again."

He must have been in terrible pain but wasn't yet showing it. No doubt he was still deadened by shock and anxiety. It seemed he didn't even know about the gash above his eye or was simply ignoring it.

Sally crawled on her hands and knees and snuggled against him. He put his arm around her and hugged her.

"Come on, sweetheart. We're not lost yet."

Mom was starting to recover now and slowly hauled herself up into a sitting position. She rubbed the back of her head.

"I seem to have gotten away with it, too," she said, between bouts of coughing. "I think I knocked myself out on the roof of the bunk when *Quintana* went over. How did I get out here?"

"We'll tell you all about that later. We're not out of the woods yet. If we're all mobile, which we seem to be, we'd better get to work. *Quintana*'s barely a live ship.

We've got to get her higher in the water. The pump handles are below water level, so there's only one thing for it. We'll have to bail for all we're worth for the next few hours, and in the meantime hope another wave doesn't come along. I doubt we'd survive another."

"I know where the buckets are," said Sally, getting to her feet. Then a look of dismay flickered across her face. "At least I know where they were," she added quietly. "They were just below us, under the prow, in the cupboard next to the head."

"They'll still be there, surely," Andy replied. "This part of the deck is still intact. I would guess we only lost things from the galley when the doghouse got ripped off."

He swung his legs over the edge of the hatch and started to lower himself down into the water.

"I'll see if they're there," he said.

"Be careful," Peter Thompson called as he was descending. "There'll be all sorts of things loose down there now. Don't get snagged on anything."

"Okay."

Andy sank down once more into the

filthy water. Keeping his eyes closed, he felt his way along the bunks to the door leading into the prow area where the water tanks, the toilet, and the shower were. The door was not even on its hinges; the impact had ripped it off completely. He swam through the opening and maneuvered himself so that he was standing on top of the water tanks. They felt solid under his feet, so with any luck they would be unruptured and they would still have fresh water. Under the prow there was an air gap of about twelve inches, so he was able to surface into that and breathe. The doors were still intact, too, and he heaved a sigh of relief. The precious buckets were not lost. He opened the door and the buckets floated out toward him on the water's surface.

He called up to the others.

"It's all right. They're here. I'm bringing them up."

He grabbed two by the handles and set off back into the cabin area. They dragged heavily in the water, and it was surprisingly difficult pulling them along behind him. By the time he surfaced below the hatch, he was out of breath again.

"Here," he gasped, handing them up through the hatch.

Hands reached down and took them from him, and he hauled himself once more up onto deck.

"Give me one, Dad," Sally demanded. "You can't do that one-handed."

She snatched a bucket from him and started to walk back along the deck to the stern.

"I'll start in the cockpit," she said.

"And I'll start here," replied Andy as he emerged through the hatch.

They plunged their buckets into the water and started to bail.

The amount of water they removed and threw over the side with those first two buckets was tiny.

But as they turned and bent to fill the buckets for the second time, a single thought struck Andy and Sally simultaneously. They both paused, frozen in midaction. They looked at each other and grinned.

Neither spoke. There was no need to speak.

They held each other's eyes for a second,

then they simply bent, refilled their buckets, and continued.

Their parents, sitting holding each other dazedly on the deck, saw the look and read their minds.

The simple action of throwing those first small amounts of water over the side was a powerful symbol.

It was the first step in their battle for survival.

FOURTEEN

&

It took two hours of continuous bailing before they were certain. At first it seemed to make no difference at all, and they began to suspect that *Quintana*'s hull had been holed so that she was taking in water as fast as they were getting rid of it.

But gradually it became apparent that she was indeed rising. By eleven o'clock about twelve inches of her hull was showing above sea level, and the water level inside her had fallen sufficiently to expose the pump handles.

Everyone began to feel much happier.

Quintana would survive. She had saved them again.

"Just as well," Peter Thompson announced to the family when everyone started to relax. "I don't know whether any of you noticed, but the dinghy's gone. We had no escape anyway if *Quintana* had been sunk."

Everyone had noticed, but nobody had said anything about it.

Peter Thompson went below, and standing waist-deep in a foul mixture of water, diesel fuel, sodden papers, and floating food and vegetables, succeeded, one-handed, in fastening rubber hoses to the pumps. He fed the hoses out through the hatches, and Andy and Sally abandoned the bucketing and started the equally laborious job of pumping. Soon water was gushing satisfyingly out onto deck and running away through the drain holes. Now and then one of them would curse as a pump became blocked with some piece of debris, and there would be a grumbling pause as the offending object was prized out.

In the first hour there had been little time to assess the extent of the disaster. Keeping *Quintana* afloat had been their only thought. Now, as the immediate dangers began to recede, there was time to take stock.

Quintana was desperately hurt. Both masts were gone. The mizzenmast had vanished entirely, ripped from its seating and carried away by the wave. The mainmast had sheared off at deck level and was broken into four pieces. It was floating, tangled in a web of wire shrouds and shredded sail, to leeward. Only one of the shrouds was still attached to the deck, but that had been enough to stop the mast from floating away.

The rudder had vanished, too, and the heavy brass wheel lay in the bottom of the cockpit well. It was twisted and buckled beyond recognition.

So they had no wind power and no steering.

And it emerged, as the water level inside *Quintana* fell, that there would be no motor power, either. Incredibly, the engine was gone. Not just moved. Not just in a different position. Gone completely.

"Good Lord!" said Peter Thompson, astonished, when Andy drew his attention to it. "I don't believe it."

He stared down onto the empty engine mountings.

"It weighed over a ton."

He shook his head, incredulously. "Imagine. If that thing had hit any of us . . ."

"That accounts for the missing dog-house," Sally called, continuing to pump. "When *Quintana* rolled, the engine came adrift and fell straight through the ship. It took the galley floor and doghouse with it."

The yawning hole in the deck suggested that she was right.

"Well, good riddance to it, anyway. It's now where it always deserved to be. I'd often thought of throwing it overboard."

Andy grinned. "Yes, Dad, you've made that obvious over the years."

Peter Thompson got down on his hands and knees, wincing with the pain from his shoulder, and inspected the engine bay. There was still a lot of water there and he had to grope around under the surface.

"At least it's broken away cleanly," he said after a while. "The propshaft's still here. If the engine hadn't broken away where it did, it might have pulled the propeller through the hull. We'd definitely have sunk then. We've been very lucky."

"The engine going like that might have been a blessing anyway." Ann Thompson appeared down the galley steps. "That extra

151

weight might have been the last straw for *Quintana*. She was so low I can't believe she stayed floating anyway."

"How are you, Mom?" Andy asked.

"I'm fine now. I've recovered. Time I did some work. I think I should do some pumping. You go up above and see what needs doing up there."

"Right. Mind where you step. There's all sorts of things rattling about down there under the water."

"And I'll take over from Sally for the moment. You only need one arm to pump, so I'm the ideal candidate." Peter Thompson grimaced ruefully. He had put a wad of torn sail under his armpit and then tied his arm tightly to his chest to pull his shoulder out and relieve the pressure on his broken collarbone. He must have been in great pain but concealed it with jokes.

"At least it's the same shoulder as last time, dear," Mom pointed out. "You'll still be able to play your silly game and embarrass us all."

Sally handed over her pump to her father. She emerged on deck through the hatch at the same time as Andy came up the galley steps. She began to walk back toward Andy.

"Mind how you go, Sal. The deck's very greasy from the oil."

"I'm all right," she replied, picking her way carefully over the tangle of stanchions and wires.

She joined her brother and they stood surveying the sad scene.

Things looked very desolate. The sky was beginning to darken now, as the smoke from the volcano spread toward them. The gloomy light gave things a depressing hue.

Up to that moment neither of them had given much thought to what had happened.

The urgency of activity, the adrenaline pumping through them as they battled to lift poor *Quintana,* had filled their minds. They had looked around, of course, as they had been bailing, but only brief, fleeting glances.

Down below, working at the pumps, they had been able to see much of the chaos that had been wrought inside the boat. Cupboards were smashed, bunks twisted, floorboards torn away. Books, oranges, loaves of bread, charts, all floating in filthy water, were sodden and ruined.

But mostly these were small things. Damage of the sort you would expect in a roll. And in a way they had known what to expect. They'd been knocked about and rolled before.

Admittedly Andy and Sally had both been small when *Quintana* had last been dismasted, off the African coast, but they both had vivid memories of it.

Neither would ever forget the sickening feeling when a ship reaches the point of no return and begins to keel over, the terrible moment when you realize that your ceiling has become your floor, and the interminable, hourlike seconds as you wait for your ship to right itself again. Or the destruction that can be caused to a ship in a few, brief violent seconds.

But nothing had prepared them for the sheer power that had caused this damage.

The mainmast was not only broken off, it was shattered into pieces: a fifty-foot, solid trunk snapped like a matchstick.

"Just look at that," she added. "I didn't notice it before. The mast is all broken up."

"I know. And look at this."

Andy picked up the tortured metal that had been the wheel.

"That's solid brass. Just look at it. You'd have needed a hammer and vise and about half an hour to get it into that shape."

"It looks like tangled yarn," observed Sally.

And as their eyes passed over *Quintana*'s deck they found that every metal rail stanchion was bent over, flattened to the deck, and the wire hawsers of the rails were broken.

"What happened exactly, do you know?"

"I think we tripped," Andy replied.

"Tripped? What do you mean?"

"Tripped. Just like tripping up. Getting your toe caught."

Sally looked uncomprehendingly at him.

"Look. I think what happened was this: When the tidal wave got up close to us, it picked up *Quintana*'s stern. I can remember looking right down toward the bow, as though *Quintana* was standing on end, nearly vertical. Then I think she slipped down so that her bow went under water. The wave continued pushing her in the stern and she just flipped over. Head over heels. Tripped over."

"I've never heard of a ship doing that before."

"Neither have I. But that could be because no one's lived through it to tell about it before."

"Mmm. Perhaps. I guess we wouldn't have survived in anything but *Quintana*. She really is remarkable. I feel so sorry for her. It's like having someone in the family badly injured."

"I know. Anyway, enough standing about. It's time we did some more work."

He called down through the gaping hole where the doghouse had been.

"Dad. What do you think we should do about the mast? Shall I just cut it free?"

"I was thinking about that," the reply came back. "The mast will be no use. It's too broken. See if there's any sign of the boom. We might be able to make a jury rig with it. Haul everything up to the side and we'll see what's what."

"Right. Come on, Sal. Let's heave it all over here."

Together they took hold of the single remaining attached shroud and started to pull. The heavy canvas was waterlogged. Knotted and folded around the mast, it resisted their efforts. They struggled and heaved and the slim wire bit into their hands painfully. Eventually it started to give; the tangled mass began to inch toward them.

"Ouch." Andy stopped pulling and inspected his hand. It was bleeding from a deep slice in the palm. He sucked at it.

"Watch your hands, Sal. The wire's shredded in places."

"Yes. I see it."

It was ten minutes before the debris was alongside.

"Here," called Dad. "I've found the toolbox. It was wedged down in the bilges. You'll need to cut some of the shrouds."

He passed the toolbox up through the hole. Andy dragged it up to the prow and set about trying to sort out the mess. Kneeling on deck, he systematically snipped away at the wire shrouds with bolt cutters while Sally, kneeling beside him, dragged pieces of sail aboard as they came free. Now and then they would gasp with pain as salt water splashed into the open wounds on their legs and hands.

It was difficult and strenuous work and they were soon sweating profusely. The day was rapidly becoming more and more oppressive and heat laden as the black cloud spread across the sky toward them. Now and then they would glance anxiously up to assess its progress. Worried, they could see flashes of lightning ripping violently through it. The tremendous heat pouring up into the sky would be creating huge turbulence, literally altering the climate.

They tried to work more quickly.

"Andy, I need a hand with this." Sally was struggling with a piece of knotted sail. "There's a piece of the mast resting on top of it. Grab hold and see if we can pull it out from underneath."

Andy took hold of the sail and heaved with her. The mast rolled as the sail moved underneath it.

"Again. One. Two. Three. Pull!"

The sail moved another few inches and the mast rolled again.

"Once more and we've got it. One. Two. Three. *Pull!*"

The mast rolled right off the edge and the sail lurched toward them. They both staggered backward as it released itself.

And miraculously, with a sucking, plopping sound, the dinghy bobbed, upside down, to the surface.

Sally cheered. "Well," she said. "Will you look at that? What a stroke of luck."

"What is it?" Mom called up. "What have you found?"

"The dinghy's here," Andy shouted back. "What's more, it looks undamaged."

Dad's head appeared through the hatch. "Marvelous. Let's get it alongside."

Andy and Sally began tugging again at the tangled debris, but the dinghy had freed itself completely from everything else. It began to float gently away from them.

"Oh, no!" Sally exclaimed.

"Don't worry, I'll fetch it," Andy said, and without hesitation dived into the water.

As he struck out toward the dinghy he heard his father shout. "Watch out for yourself! Don't get caught up in the shrouds."

Andy circled around the wreckage and in a few seconds had arrived at the dinghy. He tried a couple of times to haul himself up onto it, but its fiberglass hull was slippery and he could not gain a hold.

Briefly he noticed a smear of blood on the hull. He had opened the cut in his palm again.

He abandoned his attempts to climb on and simply swam around to the back of the dinghy, took hold of its stern, and started to swim back, kicking hard with his legs. If it had been the right way up it would have been easy, but upside down the dinghy was awkward and heavy. It went every way except the way he wanted it to go.

But he pushed and tugged and maneuvered it gradually and more or less in a straight line until, after ten minutes of effort, he had it banging gently up against *Quintana*'s hull.

Sally reached down and held on to it.

Andy remained in the water. "Let's see if we can right it," he said. "See if you can find a bit of rope."

"There's some down below in the cupboard where the buckets were. I'll get it."

Andy trod water while Sally disappeared through the forward hatch. She was back quickly and passed one end of the rope down to Andy. He laid the rope across the dinghy's upturned hull, paid out about two feet extra, then submerged. Working underneath the dinghy, he quickly knotted the rope around the seat on the far side.

Then he surfaced and climbed back aboard *Quintana*. "Right, Sal. If we both give a good heave on this, we should be able to pull her over."

They both pulled strongly on the rope. The side of the dinghy slowly rose out of the water and came to the vertical. An extra-sharp pull flipped it over and it righted itself.

Sally secured it to one of the flattened stanchions.

"There," said Andy. "Thank goodness for that. I feel a good deal safer now we've got that as backup."

He sat down on the deck to rest and regain his breath. His hand was bleeding quite heavily now.

"We'll try and do something with that cut now," Sally said.

"No. Leave it. It's nothing. It'll stop

soon. Let's just get on. There's more of the sail to pull in. And I'm hoping the boom will appear somewhere among it. Now we've got the dinghy I've got an idea."

"What?"

"I'll tell you if we find the boom. For the moment I'm keeping it to myself."

Sally snorted with annoyance but decided not to pursue it. "Okay." She went back to the other side of the deck and started to haul on the wreckage again.

"Come on. Don't just sit there."

Andy joined her and they resumed their salvage operation.

Andy was right about his cut. It did soon stop bleeding.

But it had been bleeding as he swam out to the dinghy, and bleeding more heavily still as he came back.

It was nothing. Only a cut. The amount of blood he had left in the sea was tiny. Something he had hardly noticed.

But something else had noticed; had registered those tiny drops of blood; had identified and positioned them.

And now, deep under the surface of the

sea, in the half-light grayness, the shark pack had turned.

They were not interested immediately. They were gorged from feeding.

But, as they rested, drifting silently in the depths, the blood was noted and its location stored.

FIFTEEN

ৡৢ

Old Sea-bird wept quietly to himself as he stood looking at his house.

The *tsunami* had ripped it apart.

He had expected damage. In his long life he had seen many great storms, many earthquakes, and many tidal waves. When the Spirits of the Land, the Spirits of the Sea, and the Spirits of the Air go to war, then man's creations are puny beside their power.

But always in the past, his house had remained standing.

Now it was destroyed, and he wept with dismay at its destruction.

From the village the wails of the women and girls and the shouts of the men mingled with his soft crying. They, too, would be surveying their losses. But they could start again. In a day or two new houses would be going up, possessions would have been retrieved from wherever they had been swept, and life would be returning more or less to normal.

Sea-bird, as he surveyed the place that had been his home, knew that he could not start again.

His house was gone. But it wasn't the house for which Sea-bird wept. The house was wood and bamboo. Worthless. And the men would help him rebuild it anyway, he knew that. They would know he was too old now to do it himself.

No. It was more than that. Much more.

He was weeping for the life that had been lived there. For the things the house had contained. Things collected over the years, stored and handled with love and pride. Each thing a small capsule of memory, each thing carrying a small piece of time.

And time cannot be rebuilt, cannot be retrieved.

His precious shark fins, which had hung from the rafters of the house, were gone. With them had gone the days of shark calling. The battles and failures and triumphs of a life, swept away on a brief, violent wave.

Now he was no longer Old Sea-bird, the great Shark Caller.

Now, without his tokens, his trophies, he was only a tired old man stripped of his pride, sifting sadly through the broken remnants of his days.

That was why he wept.

He was confused and angry, too. In his final years the sea had beaten him.

He could not understand it.

The signs had not been bad. The magic had been performed in exactly the same way he had performed it so many times in the past. The ancestors had been called to protect the new Shark Caller; the good *masalai* sharks had been brought up from the depths, the evil speared to the ocean floor.

Everything had been done as it should have been done.

But now things were wrong. The earth was broken and spitting fire and smoke; the sky was darkening by day; the sea was churned into a maelstrom; and he had no magic to control any of these things.

The evil *masalai* were in charge. They had finally won.

He sighed deeply and looked out to sea. It was quiet again now but looked gray and ominous, as though the surface calm concealed a deep, hidden turmoil.

He feared greatly for Kaleku. The wave could already have destroyed him.

Perhaps even, he thought briefly, it would be better if it had. If the evil *masalai* sharks were abroad then nothing would save him anyway.

He quickly dismissed the thought as his anger banished his confusion. He was allowing events to take control of him, when all his life he had controlled events.

Perhaps there was no magic left. Perhaps he was just a frail old man railing against an inevitable fate. Perhaps the sea had shown him that man can never master it. But what was he to do now? Just accept things? Lie down here, on land, and die defeated?

No.

He couldn't do that.

The sea had taken almost everything away from him. But there were things remaining that the sea could never take. A lifetime of learning the ways of the shark, a store of knowledge and cunning and tactics and trickery hard-won from half a century of battles. These had not been taken away.

An idea started to form in his mind.

He looked up and down the beach, searching for his canoe. There was no sign of it.

No matter. He would find a canoe. The wave would have swept all the villagers' canoes in from the shore. Any one would do.

He had made up his mind. He would go to sea once more. He would find the sharks one final time.

No matter that his *larung* was gone; the sharks would know when Sea-bird came.

No matter that there was no *kasaman* to snare them; he still had his spear. That would be enough.

No matter that there was little hope of a weak old man ever coming back; he didn't want to come back. He just wanted to go on his terms.

He would go back to the sea to die as he had spent his life.

Hunting sharks.

He set off down the shoreline, searching for a canoe.

———

As Sea-bird was seeking a canoe, Kaleku was righting his.

It had escaped virtually undamaged, and Kaleku was proud that his preparations had paid off. The outrigger was a bit loose but, as soon as the craft was turned back over, he would be able to tighten the lashings. As far as he could tell from swimming underneath the canoe and feeling inside it, all the precious hunting things were still secure under the seats.

Tying himself to the canoe had been the wisest thing he had done, though the wave had not hit him with the violence its terrifying size had promised. But as he had expected, he had been thrown out and cartwheeled over and over in the water, gasping and choking for air.

The canoe, light as a cork, had surfed along with the wave, gradually rising up it until it bobbed through the crest. Kaleku was simply dragged, struggling, in its wake, and finally deposited some minutes later, spluttering but unharmed, beside it.

He had clung to its upturned hull for several minutes, regaining his breath and allowing his thumping heart to steady.

Now, still in the water, he had untied his securing rope from the canoe's hull and was fastening it around the outrigger. That done, he threw the remainder of the rope across the hull to the other side and swam around after it.

Turning the craft over was then very easy; he had done it many times before. He hauled himself out of the water up onto the upturned hull and stood, swaying a little to keep his balance. Then he took hold of the rope and simply leaned back, putting all his weight on the rope. The outrigger rose out of the water, quickly came to the vertical, and, as Kaleku fell backward into the sea, the canoe dropped gently into position beside him. He submerged under the hull, came up between the hull and outrigger, and climbed in once more. The whole operation took no more than a minute.

He sat quietly for a while, marveling that he had survived such a wave. At the moment that it had hit, he had been convinced that all was lost and had found his thoughts to be not on fear of death but on fear of failure.

But he was still here. Still in the game.

Perhaps things were not against him after all.

He found himself now to be strangely calm. He methodically checked that his *larung, kasaman,* and spear were still there as he had hoped. Everything was still secure where he had fastened it.

Fears and doubts were being overtaken by a growing fatalism. Whatever was going to happen, would happen, it seemed. All he could do was prepare as well as he could. This time the preparations had paid off. Next time they might or might not.

All he could do was his best. Who alive could do any more?

He sighed, picked up his paddle, and prepared to move off again, to push yet farther out into the channel.

The sharks were still waiting.

Just before he moved off, he remembered the white sail he had noticed to the southwest as the wave had approached.

He stood up and scanned the sea.

The sail was gone. The craft had not survived.

He shook his head sadly. The sea had claimed more victims.

There was nothing he could do, so he sat, plunged his paddle into the sea, and resumed his lonely search for the shark roads.

Ten miles to the east, an old man had dragged a canoe down to the water's edge, taken a last, sad look at the place that had been his home, then turned his back and resolutely paddled away on what he knew would be his final journey.

Ten miles to the west, a family battled to save a stricken ship and made nervous, hopeful plans for their survival.

Overhead, smoke turned day to night.

And under the sea, agitated by the upheavals of land and water, nervous and edgy, the sharks swirled.

SIXTEEN

⚓

What Andy and Sally had finally managed to retrieve from the sodden mass of wreckage had been carefully laid out on deck and assessed for its usefulness.

This was the list: Five good-size pieces of sail. The rest had been so ripped and shredded that it was useless, so they had cut it free and cast it adrift.

Several lengths of wire shroud. Most of it had been so tangled that Andy had had to cut it into small lengths, but he had managed to salvage one piece of about twenty meters and another just short of that.

Some assorted lengths of rope, two of them with pulleys still attached.

An assortment of pieces of wood, mostly floorboards that had been carried out by the departing engine, then trapped under the sail.

The boom, intact, and two pieces of mast about six feet long.

Now they were sitting on the cabin roof by the forward hatch, surveying their spoils.

The light had faded considerably, as the high black smoke cloud had almost reached them. The first ash was beginning to fall and *Quintana*'s deck was taking on a grayish color as the fine dust settled and clung to the oily wood.

"Not much, is it?" said Sally disappointedly. "After all that work."

"Not much. But considering the state of things, I suppose we're lucky to have this. Shut up a minute, anyway. I'm thinking."

"Hmph." She snorted disdainfully. "And I suppose the world has to stop because you're thinking."

Andy grinned. "I see you're feeling better. I was a bit worried about you. You hadn't insulted me all morning."

"I've had other things on my mind. You perhaps noticed. Like being thankful to be alive. And thankful everyone else is."

Her face clouded.

"When you think what might have happened. . . ." She trailed off.

"Don't think what might have happened. It didn't, and that's all there is to it. It's what's going to happen now that matters, and that's what I'm thinking about, if you'll give me a chance."

"Right." She fell silent and waited.

Andy got to his feet and picked up one of the larger pieces of floorboard. He studied it carefully without speaking.

Sally watched him curiously.

Ash was falling gently all the time now. It gave the air a sulfurous smell but was not thick enough to impede their breathing. Nor was it hot, because its long descent from the high atmosphere had cooled it. Sally noticed that where Andy walked he left footprints in the dust. She noticed, too, the first stirrings of a warm breeze.

Andy put down the wood and unfolded the pieces of salvaged sail. He spread each one out carefully, one on top of the other, on the cabin roof. Then, after a great deal of seemingly heart-searching consideration, he selected a piece of sail, put it to one side, and refolded the others.

Curiosity started to get the better of Sally, but she managed not to give in to it.

Andy sat down again and stared, brow furrowed, at the dinghy. He stared for a long time, occasionally nodding to himself, occasionally turning and looking at the sail, or the rope, or the boom.

Sally couldn't stand it any longer. "Oh, for goodness' sake. Stop playing the mystery man, will you? What are you up to?"

"Right. I'm thinking this out before we talk to Mom and Dad about it. This is the way I see things. We've survived and we're in no immediate danger. But *Quintana*'s immobilized. None of the sail we've salvaged is big enough to make any sort of jury rig that would be strong enough to pull her. So she's just going to drift aimlessly."

"Yes, I'd already figured that out."

"So we've two options, it seems to me. The first is we just sit here and hope something comes by that will give us a tow."

"Hmm. What are the chances of that, do you think?"

"Possible, but not likely. We're on no main shipping route at all here. The only things in these waters would be vessels heading from Rabaul up to Kavieng. Small freighters and things like that. And I don't

176

have to tell you why nothing will be coming out of Rabaul at the moment."

"What about *from* Kavieng?"

"Nothing from there, either, I shouldn't think. News of the eruption will have been radioed to there and ships will have been told not to go near Rabaul. The only things heading for New Britain now will be the navy ships that were standing by for rescue. They'll come up from the south, nowhere near us. Heaven knows how long it will take to sort out the mess at Rabaul, so we could find ourselves drifting around here for days."

"What's wrong with that? We've plenty of food and water."

"Nothing's wrong with it, provided the weather stays good. I know we're in the calm season, but no one knows what effects the eruption will have. It could well bring storms. *Quintana*'s not controllable in the state she's in. She would almost certainly be broached and swamped."

"So what's the second option?"

"The second option is to jury-rig the dinghy, and I'll go and get help."

There was a long pause while Sally

thought about it. She looked around at the huge, silent, darkening expanses of ocean surrounding them.

"From where?"

"From New Ireland."

There was another, longer pause before she gave her verdict.

"Mad," she said finally. "Completely mad. Insane. I always suspected it. I've lived seventeen years with a madman."

"Come on, Sal. Think about it. Look at the dinghy and I'll explain."

"Go on then."

"We've got the mainmast boom. This is why I was hoping we would find it. If we chisel a hole through the dinghy's seat we can slot the boom into it for a makeshift mast. We've enough rope to lash it into place. The piece of sail I've left out is about eight feet by six, just about right. Presto, we've got a sailing boat."

"The way you put it, it sounds almost possible."

"It is possible. Easily possible."

"What about steering?"

"Simple. There's a six-foot floorboard there. If we saw it roughly into an oar shape and figure out a way of fastening it to the stern of the dinghy, then we've got a steering oar."

"All right. But how will you control the sail? How will you tack if you need to? You'll have no boom."

"Those two pulleys that were still attached to the ropes we found—if we screw those onto the sides of the dinghy, I can just run a rope from the corner of the sail through one or the other. If I need to change course, I'll just release the rope from one and thread it through the other. Slow, but it will work."

Sally sighed but was impressed with the logic. "I don't know. Theory's all right. But it's an awful long way to New Ireland. It must be sixty miles at least."

"No. We were heading for Kavieng, remember. That's right at the northernmost tip of the island. I guess that to the nearest point, due east, it's probably only twenty miles. There's already a bit of breeze springing up. Twenty miles is nothing. Only a few hours, if everything goes well."

"And several thousand years dead if they don't."

Andy grinned. "You've got a way of encouraging people, haven't you? This is the only way. You know it is, so you may as well stop being cynical and help me get it organized."

"I'm not cynical, I'm practical. I suppose you know what you're doing, though. Not that it matters. You won't be doing it anyway. You've left something out of your carefully calculated equation."

"What?"

"Dad. That's what. Let me know when you're going to tell him your plan so that I can be well out of the way. I don't want my ears damaged with the bellowing."

"I can handle Dad. No problem," Andy replied firmly.

"Hmph," said Sally. "I'm impressed. Very."

The end of their conversation coincided with Peter Thompson's head appearing through the hatch.

"Right," he announced. "Your mother and I have straightened things up down here now. I think it's time for a conference. You two come down, and we'll start making some decisions about what we're going to do. I hope you've got some good ideas."

Andy glared at Sally, daring her to speak.

She put on her well-practiced "completely innocent" face.

Then they both climbed down into the cabin.

SEVENTEEN

❦

Absolutely crazy. Sail that thing? It's a rowboat, for heaven's sake. It's for rowing a hundred yards in to shore from a mooring. It hasn't even got a keelboard. You won't last ten minutes. I forbid it. Absolutely, completely forbid it."

That had been the gist of Peter Thompson's reaction to his son's idea.

There had been more, much more, most of it delivered at a volume that could have been heard a mile away. But that was what it had all boiled down to.

It was insane, suicidal, and forbidden.

Sally had a self-satisfied smirk on her face through it all. Every wrinkle of her expression said *I told you so.*

But Andy was not to be put off.

"I know all that. I know it's not going to be the steadiest boat in the world, but I have thought it out. I can keep it steady enough with the steering oar. And I learned to sail when I was about five, remember. You're not giving me credit, Dad."

"You didn't learn to sail in a tin bath, which is about as much good as that thing will be."

"Look at the alternative. We might be drifting around here for days. I know we're all right for food and water, but we don't know what's going to happen. *Quintana*'s very vulnerable like this. If we get a storm, she'll go down. Isn't it better to risk one life rather than all our lives?"

"There's no reason for any life to be risked just on the remote possibility that there might be a storm. We're safer here and safer all together. *Quintana* will cope, and we'll cope with whatever comes as it happens. Sooner or later something will come along and give us a tow."

"Maybe. But when? Look at the state of us. You've got a broken collarbone and a gashed head. How much use will you be in a storm? Sally's got no skin on her legs. They're okay now, but give them two days in this climate and they'll be festered and swollen like an elephant's. Mom knocked herself out and swallowed a gallon of water and diesel. You can't do that without some consequences. My eyes feel like they're five times their normal size. We all need attention, Dad."

"Who's the doctor here? Me or you?"

"You are. But you've nothing to doctor us with. All your first-aid stuff and drugs went out through the doghouse roof with the engine."

"We'll get by. I'm not giving in to you. It's too dangerous."

"Right. I'm not saying it's not dangerous. But it's possible, you've got to admit that. And the longer we argue about it, the more dangerous it becomes. At the moment we've got a nice breeze. But the air's heating up all the time from the volcano. By tomorrow it might be a gale. Then I won't be able to go. I've reckoned twenty miles to the New Ireland coast. With any luck I could have a rescue boat back here by tomorrow afternoon."

"If you're not at the bottom of the sea."

"I won't be. I can handle it."

"*No!*"

Andy snorted with annoyance at his father's intractability.

"At least give the idea a chance, Dad. You're dismissing it out of hand. I'll strike a bargain with you. I'll rig the dinghy and then you'll see what I mean. I'll sail it around here a bit to find out how it performs. Then we'll make the final decision. What do you say?"

Peter Thompson considered for a moment, then sighed.

"If it will keep you happy, I'll agree to that. Go on, rig it and try it. Then, perhaps, when we've fished you out of the water, you'll abandon the stupid idea."

Andy grinned. At least this was a partial victory.

"Right," he replied. "Come on, Sal, let's get to work. You start on that plank. Just cut it roughly into an oar shape, will you."

He opened the toolbox and handed her a saw.

"I'll start cutting the hole for the mast."

He sifted through the tools until he had

found a hammer and a large chisel, then jumped down into the dinghy and started to chisel away at the seat.

Peter Thompson shook his head. "Barmy," he muttered to himself.

But he was smiling as he said it. If he had been truthful with Andy, he would have admitted that he was very proud of his children. They had suffered an appalling catastrophe and emerged from it magnificently. There had not been one word of complaint or recrimination or self-pity. They had simply gotten on with what had to be done and were still doing so.

And now, he realized, his blusterings and bellowings were probably not going to work.

Every father comes to a point in life where he realizes that his children are no longer in his control, no longer dependent on him to protect them. This, he guessed, as he watched his daughter sawing away at a length of wood with determined concentration and his son whacking away happily at a chisel, was that point. He wasn't watching his children at all. The children were gone. These two people were a man and a woman working together for survival.

What's more, they were doing exactly what he would have done if he had been able.

Andy was right, this was the best way.

Perhaps it was time to let go.

He crossed to where Sally was struggling to hold the plank steady while she sawed it.

"Er," he said, "if I put my foot on that, it'll make it a bit easier for you."

Sally smiled to herself but said nothing.

A few seconds later she caught Andy's eye and winked.

They knew they had won.

"Talk about Heath Robinson. I've never seen anything like it."

"It doesn't matter what it looks like, Dad. It's how it performs that matters."

"Yes, and I've got some idea about that, too."

"Come on, Dad, admit it. It's brilliant," retorted Sally.

"I agree," said Mom. "I think it's marvelous."

They had finished and were proudly admiring their work. The dinghy was transformed.

They had sawed an eight-foot length off the boom. This had slotted neatly through the hole in the seat and had made an acceptable mast. It was lashed firmly to the seat, and Andy had fastened a block of wood underneath to stop the mast from moving. Sally had nailed the canvas to the mast and cut it roughly to a triangular shape. It was an untidy but workable sail. The two pulleys had been nailed to the sides of the dinghy and a length of rope fastened to the corner of the sail so Andy could pull it tight or release it at will for maneuverability. Dad had rigged the sea oar by simply cutting a hole high up in the dinghy's sternboard and pushing the oar's handle through from the back. He had wound strips of torn sail around the handle, which both made it more comfortable to hold and, more importantly, stopped the oar from slipping back through the hole and becoming lost. As an added precaution, he had tied a length of rope from the handle to the mast. If the oar did pull through the hole, it wouldn't then be able to drift away.

"I'm admitting nothing. It's a death trap."

"Well, I've got confidence in it," said Andy, undeterred. "Sea trials now. I'll take her out, and we'll see what happens."

Sally sat down on the deck and untied the rope that secured the dinghy to *Quintana*.

"Say when you're ready," she said, "and I'll push you off."

"Right, one second," Andy replied.

He took the direction of the wind, threaded the sail rope through the starboard pulley, but left the sail flapping loosely. He sat down in the stern and grasped the steering oar.

"Okay, Sal," he said. "Go."

She pushed the dinghy off with her foot, and it began to drift gently away. It rolled a little from side to side, even with the sail unfilled. The weight of the mast unsteadied it severely. Andy groaned inwardly. Perhaps it wasn't going to work after all.

Gingerly, a couple of inches at a time, he started to draw in the sail rope, tightening the sail. As it began to fill, the dinghy started to heel, so he scrambled up and sat on the port edge, leaning out so that his weight counteracted the heel. The dinghy steadied, and he drew in more of the rope. The sail gradually filled more, and the dinghy heeled more. He was now unable to push the steering oar with his hand. He couldn't lean outward to give the dinghy weight and lean inward to steady the oar at the same time. He tried pushing the oar with his foot, and the dinghy began to turn and heel even more. The port side was now coming up too far, and he was in danger of capsizing.

He let the sail rope go. It slithered through the pulley, and the sail loosened and flapped uselessly against the mast. The dinghy splashed down again into the water and pendulumed from side to side.

Andy was desperately disappointed. He had known it wasn't going to be steady, but this was impossible. He was barely twenty yards from *Quintana* and already had nearly capsized.

"No good," he called back. "I nearly went over then and I hadn't even gotten the sail properly filled. We need a small rethink."

He unwound the canvas from the oar handle, pulled it out through the stern, and paddled the dinghy back to *Quintana*'s side.

Everyone looked very despondent.

"I told you," Peter Thompson said. "You can't sail a thing like that without a keelboard. And there's no way of fitting one."

"Well, we'll have to think of something else then, won't we? Think, everyone," Andy ordered as he climbed back aboard and secured the dinghy again.

There was a long silence.

"You know those sailboard things that everyone had in Rabaul," Sally ventured. "They just had a slot cut in the base and a keelboard pushed through. Could we make something like that out of one of the cabin doors?"

"No," said Andy. "I doubt it. If we cut a slot in this dinghy it would ship too much water. The sailboards are just that—boards. The water just runs off them."

Eventually it was Mom who had the idea.

"Canoes don't have keelboards," she suggested. "The native canoes here, I mean. I've watched them. They seem very stable. They have outriggers."

"Aha," said Andy. "That's worth thinking

about. What have we got left that we can use?"

"We've the two pieces of broken main-mast. If we could think of a way of fastening them onto the dinghy they might do," said Sally, brightening up again. "They might be a bit heavy, though."

"The heavier the better. How much of the boom was left after we cut the mast piece?" asked Dad.

"About ten or twelve feet, I think. I'll go and get it."

She crossed to the other side of the deck.

"There's all this wire shroud left, too. We didn't use any of that. Is that any use?" asked Dad.

"How about this?" said Andy. "If we lay the rest of the boom across the dinghy and lash it well to the mast and the rowlocks, we can fasten the pieces of mainmast onto each end. Two outriggers. One on each side. A trimaran, in fact."

"I'm beginning to think you all live in a complete fantasy world," said Peter Thompson heavily. "A trimaran now, for goodness' sake. And I'm as mad as the rest of you for going along with it. Come on then, let's get it made."

Half an hour later the dinghy was pushed off for its second sea trial.

By now it was a very strange hybrid indeed: a rowboat pretending to be a sailboat, pretending to be a Pacific canoe, pretending to be a trimaran.

But whatever its pretense, the difference in the way it handled was astonishing. The outriggers were totally successful, and from the moment that he started to let the sail fill for the first time, Andy knew that the plan had become a reality.

He swung the steering oar this way and that and the boat turned, without heeling and without fuss. She was steerable and steady.

There were cheers from *Quintana* as it became apparent that their idea had paid off. And even louder cheers as Andy became more and more confident and eventually swung the little boat completely around and started to tack back toward them.

There was a huge, delighted grin on his

face as he arrived back at *Quintana*'s side.

"There," he said. "Eat your words, Dad."

"I will. Gladly. It certainly looked very seaworthy from here. How did it feel?"

"Excellent. Very steady. That's about a five-knot wind now, and it gave her no trouble at all. She handles beautifully. If I get under way immediately, I'll be within sight of land in a couple of hours."

"Oh," said Mom worriedly. "I didn't think you were going right away. Wouldn't it be better to wait until morning?"

"No. We don't know what morning will bring. Conditions are fine now. They might not be tomorrow. And, anyway, sailing at night might even be better. I'll be able to see lights from the villages."

"What if you can't see lights? How will you keep your bearings then? The compass is gone."

"Simple. The volcanoes. They're going to be raging for goodness knows how long. If it falls dark on me before I've made landfall, I'll be able to see the glow from them. They're to the southwest, so I can easily keep an easterly course with them to rely on."

"I don't suppose there's any point in trying to dissuade you, is there?" asked Peter Thompson.

"None whatever. I'm going and that's that."

"I didn't think so."

Peter gathered up the remaining pieces of rope and dropped them into the bottom of the dinghy.

"You might need those," he said. "And you'd better take some tools in case you need to do some repairs."

He handed a hammer, a chisel, and the saw down to Andy.

"Just wait a second and I'll get you some water," added Mom. "There's a plastic container in the galley that I filled from the tanks earlier."

She descended into the galley and passed up the water. Sally took it from her and handed it down into the dinghy.

"There's a couple of tins of corned beef here as well. Take those. You don't need an opener for them. That's about all there is that's of any use to you, I think."

"See if you can find me a pan, Mom. I may need to bail."

"Yes, there's one here. Battered but usable." She passed it up and it followed the rest of the things into the boat.

"That's enough now. I don't want any more weight than I need."

He stowed everything under the seat, packing it around the base of the mast.

"Right. That's it. I'm ready."

Just for a second there was an awkward pause as everybody wondered what to say. But Andy forestalled any problem.

"Right, that's it. I'm off. And before anybody says anything, I don't want any fuss. This little boat's fine. She'll get me there, no problem. I'll see you all tomorrow, or the next day at the latest."

And with that he pushed himself off.

There were no "good-byes" or "good lucks." There was no need for things like that.

Everyone, especially Andy, knew the risks. Everyone knew that the sea could change at whim. There was nothing to be done about that. The boat was as good as they could make it, and Andy was as good a sailor as anyone.

So there was simply silence as he turned

his back on his family and his home, pointed the tiny dinghy's prow toward the east, allowed the sail to fill to billowing, and pulled smoothly and strongly away.

EIGHTEEN

❧

It's probably only about twenty miles.

Those words, spoken so glibly when he had been telling Sally his plan, were now echoing hauntingly inside Andy's head.

Twenty miles is nothing. Only a few hours, if things go well.

Things were going well, after a fashion. The makeshift rig was pulling the little craft along in a warm, steady breeze.

But now, an hour into his journey, he found that the increasing gloom as the sky continued to darken was beginning to unsettle him. Logic told him that there was little to fear from it. The falling ash posed no threat and there was no sign yet of any increase in the wind, which might presage a storm.

Really there was nothing to worry about.

But, nevertheless, he found that he was still worried.

The first mile had been the most anxious. His eyes had flicked constantly around the boat. Would the block of wood steadying the base of the mast hold? Were the lashings on the outriggers tight enough and would he be able to refasten them if they worked loose? If there was a sudden squall, would he be able to jibe quickly enough? If the wind increased, would the sail hold or would it tear away from the mast? All these things persistently gnawed at his mind and his confidence.

At first it had been the noises that had made him anxious.

The edge of the sail flapped like wet washing in a wind. The steering oar clattered in its hole in the sternboard, an irritating, rhythmless drum rattle. The base of the mast banged ceaselessly against the block. At each wave the outriggers gave out a harsh, nerve-grating screech as the wire lashings bit deeply into the wood.

It all niggled away at Andy's confidence, for every sound pointed to one inescapable fact. Nothing was as tight as it should be. Nothing was really secure.

And yet here he was, after an hour of

worried vigilance, still sailing along. Nothing had come loose, nothing had fallen apart.

Why, then, he asked himself, was he now so agitated? Why did he continue to be so anxious?

The possibility of failure had hardly crossed his mind as he had thought the plan through back on *Quintana*. Sally's sarcasm and his father's blusterings had not dented his confidence at all. There was nothing reckless about what he had done. He had assessed the risks and taken the steps to control them.

But now, for some unaccountable, deeply annoying reason, he did not feel completely confident. Nothing had happened, but he had the gnawing feeling that something would.

Perhaps, he thought, it was just reality catching up. Perhaps in all the feverish activity after the capsize there had been no time to think of what might have been, or what might be yet to come. They had been too busy keeping *Quintana* afloat at first to do much thinking. But now that he was not busy, there was little to do but check that the boat was all right and monitor his course. Now there was time for doubts to creep in.

And time, too, for loneliness.

He gazed around at the sea and for the first time in his life, felt frightened of it. It was the strangest of feelings. The sea had been part of his life since his earliest memory. He thought no more about it than he thought of the land when he was upon that. Both were just there, and you lived your life upon them, enjoying their calms and respecting their storms.

When people spoke of "the cruel sea," it made him laugh. The sea is not cruel—it is neutral. Terrible things may happen in it, or on it, but the sea has no character, it is simply *there.*

But though he had traveled all the seas of the earth, there was now one difference. He had never before been alone.

Suddenly he felt very tiny, very vulnerable, and very much alone.

He shuddered at this shocking transformation as he realized the truth of his position. He was alone in an immense, darkening plain of water. Alone in a creaking, fragile mockery of a boat. A boat that the sea could suck in and spit out contemptuously in a thousand fragments.

In a single, horrifying moment the sea lost its neutrality and, against all Andy's logic and instincts, assumed a character. In a stroke it became forbidding, oppressive, and alien. Threat loomed in every wave as Andy realized how little he knew about the sea. How little anyone knew about the sea.

He became acutely conscious of the depths below him and the thinness of the floor that separated him from them.

For a second he panicked, released the sail rope so the sail flapped loosely, and jumped to his feet. He turned and looked to the southwest, hoping that he would still be able to see *Quintana*. He felt that if he could just see something, some evidence of life in this terrible, unnaturally darkened wilderness, then it would be something to hold on to. But it was a forlorn hope; he knew that even as he turned. *Quintana* would have been out of sight half an hour ago.

He turned back, took hold of the mast, and stood up on the seat, straining his eyes to see if he could see the coast of New Ireland. That was hopeless, too, as he had known it would be. New Ireland was still hours away.

He slumped back down onto the floor of the boat. His panic reaction had not only been futile, it had made things worse, emphasized his loneliness. He put his head in his hands and willed himself to stop trembling.

The words came back to haunt him again.

Only twenty miles.

Suddenly it seemed a thousand.

Only a few hours, if everything goes well.

Suddenly a few hours seemed forever.

And though he tried desperately to block out the next words, they came anyway, echoing over and over in his brain.

And several thousand years dead if they don't.

It was many minutes before he brought his emotions under control, before he found himself able to stop whimpering and trembling.

Then, naturally, he was ashamed.

"Pathetic," he snorted eventually. "How pathetic. Sniveling like a baby. Get a grip on yourself."

He avoided looking at the sea, staring down into the bottom of the boat instead.

Gradually he started to regain his composure. Whatever had brought on the crazy thoughts passed.

Then, when he felt ready, he raised his head and faced the sea once more. He threaded the sail rope through the port pulley, and the boat began to pull away.

He remained annoyed with himself and what he saw as his childishness for a long time, but gradually, over the next mile, his confidence returned. The daunting distance shortened and time regained its normal span. *Only twenty miles, only a few hours,* meant what it said again. The journey, undistorted by fear, resumed its possibility.

The wind began to strengthen to about six knots, and the little craft pulled along strongly and dependably. The groans and creaks and rattles and screams continued and seemed louder. Andy wedged his foot against the block holding the bottom of the mast and succeeded in quieting the knocking from there. The other noises he just tried to ignore. He wasn't worried about them now anyway. If nothing had broken so far, then it probably wouldn't.

He concentrated hard on staying on course and resolved to keep other things out of his mind.

The drum rattle from the steering oar got on his nerves a bit, but there was nothing he could do about that. The handle had to be loose in the hole so he could maneuver it. Every time he pushed the oar one way or the other, the handle would chatter across the hole in the sternboard, its sound amplified by the hollow hull of the boat.

Tap, tap, tap it would go, as he hauled to starboard.

Thud, thud, thud, as he pulled to port.

But he got used to it and hardly even noticed it after a time.

He did not know, and indeed would never know, that, by strange chance, in this small corner of the vast Pacific Ocean, the sound made by his oar exactly mimicked another sound.

A sound very common to these waters.

The sound of the *larung*.

And deep, deep beneath him, silent gray shapes stirred, turned, sightless in the dark currents, and began their long rise to the surface.

NINETEEN

ঐঠ

At the end of the second hour of his journey, Andy thought he could just discern a faint line of white on the northeast horizon. Etched between the cold gunmetal of the sea and the darkening sky, the line gave him heart.

It was, he hoped, the ever-present cloud bank hanging over the mountains of New Ireland.

As his boat rose to the top of each long wave, the line would rise into view, shimmer briefly, distorted by distance and the half-light, then slip down into the sea as he descended.

Eventually he was sure that it was really there and not just a trick of the light. His goal was almost in sight. Not landfall exactly, more like cloudfall.

At the same time the vague, disturbing

feeling he had had since leaving *Quintana* resolved itself.

Slowly he had become aware that his unease had nothing to do with doubts about the safety of his craft. It had soon become obvious that it would serve him well. But no matter how much he had tried to convince himself that everything was all right, he had remained unsettled and anxiously watchful.

There was nothing tangible to account for it, nothing he could put his finger on to explain it. But something was there; he knew that. Something just beyond his vision, just out of reach of his mind.

At first he had tried to dismiss the feeling. It was exhaustion, he told himself, or his overwrought imagination playing tricks. But it had persisted and grown in strength until it was undeniable. It permeated the air, rose like a dank mist of foreboding from the sea.

He was being followed. He knew it.

And at the end of the second hour, he was proved right. Drawn by the sound of the oar rattle, drawn by some ancient and inescapable urge that its sound evoked, the first grim black dorsal fin surfaced silently behind him, and a single, blankly malignant eye fixed his small boat in its sights.

Two miles to the east, Kaleku ceased paddling.

His arms ached now. The afternoon hours had brought with them an increasing wind, hot and ash-laden, from the southwest, where the volcanoes hurled their fires of rage into the sky. Kaleku had wearied with the constant battle to keep plowing west toward the shark roads.

But now, thankfully, he felt that the sea beneath his canoe had changed. It was a small change but unmistakable. His prow swung slightly north and the agitated chop of the sea tempered into a longer, lazier swell.

Kaleku knew that he had arrived. He was in a shark road.

He laid his paddle down in the bottom of the canoe and rested, allowing the craft to drift with the current. First he must gather his strength. Allow his complaining muscles to relax.

Now that the moment was upon him, he was completely calm. Doubts, fears, thoughts of success or failure were of no importance.

Now there was only him and his destiny. And his destiny waited in the depths below him, waited for his call.

The minutes passed and took the pain from his arms and shoulders. He felt his strength return.

Then he began to lay out his equipment. He examined each piece as he did so, checking that the wave had not damaged anything. The spear he placed to his right, where his hand could fall on it without his eyes needing to locate it. The snare went to his left.

Then he picked up the *larung*, plunged it into the water, and shook it.

Come, shark, come, he heard it sing.

Come, shark, come.

At first Andy was not afraid.

Sharks do follow boats. Everyone who sails is well used to that.

So when he first noticed the ominous

black fin knifing through the sea behind him, he gave it little thought.

He guessed that the shark was simply investigating.

Even when the fin was joined by another and another, though wary, he felt no fear.

There was nothing to fear from a shark pack unless you were in the water.

But the wariness began to change to a dull tremble in the pit of his stomach as more of the black triangles slid up through the surface and settled on the same course as the first.

Soon there seemed to be little doubt. They were keeping a constant distance between them and the boat. As though they were holding back, letting him pace them, as more and more caught up and joined the pack.

As though, it occurred to Andy, *they were massing to attack.*

As soon as the thought crossed his mind, he scoffed at it. It was too ridiculous. Fish have hardly ever been known to attack boats. It was almost unheard of.

But then he took another look.

The pack was still there, grown now to about a dozen, still holding back, still pursuing the same course as he.

He had to modify his self-mockery.

Hardly ever is not the same as *never.*

Almost unheard of.

Almost.

It jolted sharply into his mind that a family had been adrift at sea in a tiny dinghy for over a month after their forty-three-foot schooner had been holed and sunk by killer whales off the Galapagos Islands. The whales, thinking they were under threat from the ship, had hit it with what the family had described as "sledgehammer blows of incredible force."

Incredible force, indeed, to destroy a forty-three-foot oceangoing schooner.

He turned and looked back again at the sharks. The tremble in his stomach turned to a shock of fear.

The pack had increased to about twenty. They remained at exactly the same distance as before. It was eerie and deeply disturbing.

A forty-three-foot schooner!

What chance did he stand if they were planning to attack?

And as he watched, something yet more disquieting happened.

As though twenty creatures simultaneously obeyed a single command, the grim phalanx of black fins erupted with startling, shocking violence out from the center, as if a huge explosion had blasted the pack apart. The pack radiated outward, each fin on an arrow-straight course of its own. And as they went, they slid, in one coordinated, balletic plunge, beneath the water.

So smooth, so entirely without effort was the whole maneuver that not the smallest ripple was left behind.

The pack just vanished.

In the smallest fraction of a second, the sharks were gone.

Andy drew in breath sharply at the efficiency of the action. It was an action that spoke of awesome power and control. Even now, as he began to sense the imminence of great danger, he could not help feeling admiration mingled with his fear.

But in the desolate silence that now followed he learned true terror. The presence of the sharks had been formidable and fearful. But he had known where they were, had been able to watch their movements.

Their sudden absence was the most chilling thing he had ever known. No matter what horrors man is faced with, if he can see them he can deal with them. The horrors of the imagination are infinitely worse.

The next minute was the longest of his life as he waited, eyes anxiously scanning the empty sea. Waited for the shattering crash as the pack roared up from the depths and hit his frail craft. Waited for a great, ugly-toothed mouth to rear up through the floor.

Sledgehammer blows of incredible force.

He waited and waited. It seemed as though time had stopped. As though his heart had stopped.

But what he feared didn't happen.

Silently the machine surfaced, its component parts sliding gracefully into well-rehearsed positions.

Andy gasped. He was surrounded. Twenty menacing black sails silhouetted starkly against the gray desolation of the sea, in perfect automaton formation.

A killing machine.

For a moment he was numbed by the

shock. The sail rope slipped unnoticed from his fingers and the sail slackened. He slumped down against the sternboard, trembling with fear, and put his head in his hands, defeated.

They were going to attack, there was no doubt.

Why? There was no reason for it. He posed no threat. He had injured nothing. There was no blood to attract them. Why had they come?

Suddenly it all seemed so unfair. The Thompsons had experienced an appalling catastrophe and lived through it. And now, at the last moment, death was reaching out again, claiming him back. Reaching out when land and safety were only a few hours away, within sight. It was unjust.

The boat, sailless now, drifted aimlessly on the swells. Andy made no attempt to guide her. What was the point? There was no escape if the sharks chose to attack.

He raised his head and looked out at them again. Now that the boat had come to rest they seemed unsettled and swirled about in patternless, senseless motion. He could see heads breaking the surface of the bow waves they pushed before them. Heads that seemed to search for direction, search for him.

He recognized now what they were. Some were so close that he could see their jaws opening and closing in anticipation as they swam. They were mako sharks, the fastest and most terrible of all. The most efficient eating machines on earth.

His blood ran cold at the sight of their mouths.

They were swimming haphazardly now, circling out in long, sweeping arcs, spinning rapidly, and returning. The water behind each turned white, thrashed into foam by the enormous strength of their tails. At each spurt of speed their ugly heads rose out of the water, like the bows of speedboats surfing through the waves.

For a moment Andy thought that they were losing interest in him, that their attention had been caught by something else.

But it was a vain hope.

Gradually it became obvious that their motion was taking on direction again, resolving into a pattern.

Perhaps their movements were part of

an ancient hunting ritual, a hideous dance choreographed to confuse their prey. Who could know what motives drove these implacable creatures to do what they did? But whatever they were doing, one thing was apparent. On each inward arc they approached closer to the boat.

Andy watched with a terrible fascination. Almost as a bird is hypnotized into immobility by a snake, he found himself paralyzed by this deeply threatening display. He was at the center of a churning wheel, with lithe black death sliding in on him from every point as the fins knifed down and back, slicing the radii of the circle.

And so they advanced, closer all the time.

His mind whirled at the pointlessness of it all. Why had they chosen him? What use was the tiny speck of life called Andy Thompson to them? What horrible trick of fate had brought them here to him?

He would never know.

Soon he would be gone. Vanished from the face of the earth in a few violent seconds of whirling bodies and snapping, hideous jaws.

Gone.

With nothing left behind but the wreckage of his tiny boat bobbing gently in a sea stained red with his lifeblood.

Blood.

The word lodged on the edge of his screaming brain, trying to push its way through his fear into his consciousness.

Blood.

He desperately tried to calm his mind. His eyes flicked rapidly around the well of the boat. Perhaps there was a way. Perhaps there was an escape. If he could injure one of them, if he could draw blood, that would distract them. The pack would turn on the injured beast and feed on it.

Quickly. Quickly.

They were almost on him now. The first of the fins were sliding, hissing past him, less than six feet from the boat.

Quickly.

His eyes came to rest on the chisel lying by the base of the mast. He leapt forward and swept it up into his hand. The hard metal gleamed. He knelt down at the stern of the boat and tried to steady himself. He was shaking almost uncontrollably now.

Steady. Steady. It has to be right. It has to draw blood. One mistake and everything is lost.

A black body swished past, less than four feet away.

He waited.

Another. Still out of reach.

Another. And another. And another.

Each a few inches closer.

He could smell them now, a fetid, rank stench of sea-rotted carrion and death. He gagged and retched at the foulness of it.

He pressed his thighs against the sternboard to brace himself and took hold of it with his left hand. Any second now and one of them would be close enough. He raised the chisel high with his right arm and waited, poised to strike.

Careful now. Get it right. There's one chance only. One chance. If you lose the chisel it's the end.

He found now that he had stopped trembling and his fear had been replaced with a cold anger. Adrenaline coursed through his body, clearing his head and giving him strength.

He kept his eyes fixed on the small piece

of sea at his stern but from the corner of his eye watched the great fins sliding into his vision from his left. The moment had to be judged exactly. There was only a split second between the fin approaching and the body whooshing past him.

He made two or three mock attacks.

Wait for the fin. Hit.

The chisel snapped down, stabbing air, as a body slid past.

Wait for the fin. Hit.

The sharks were within reach now, passing less than two feet away.

Now. Next time. Do it.

He grasped the sternboard tightly and leaned out over the sea.

Wait for the fin.

It slid into his vision.

Now. HIT!

His arm arced down, all the strength of his body behind it, the steel blade of the chisel scything through the air.

He hit the shark just in front of the dorsal. He felt the chisel drive deep through flesh and grind against bone. Then it was wrenched violently from his hand, almost dragging him from the boat.

He fell, shaking, against the mast.

He had done it.

Now, what would happen?

At first nothing happened. He looked around and the shark pack was still circling and arcing toward him as it had been before. They were all very close now. The water seemed filled with fins.

His heart sank.

Nothing had changed. Perhaps the wound had been too slight to be noticed by the pack. Perhaps too slight even to have been noticed by the shark itself.

He could not even identify which of the sharks he had hit. There was no blood to be seen.

It was more than a minute before the injured beast reappeared, but when it did, the whole picture changed.

With a startling suddenness the sea erupted about fifty yards to the stern. The injured shark emerged, rising vertically through the surface. Its entire body left the water and rose up into the air, spinning madly on an axis of pain. Its hideous mouth was opened in a silent scream of agony as it whirled upward toward the sky.

Then, with a tremendous thump, it crashed down again onto the surface of the sea and submerged.

Andy held his breath. The circling pack had slowed, its attention arrested by the sound. The moving fins came to a stop, turned, and then began to slide slowly in its direction.

The wounded beast roared out through the surface again, its body twisting frantically. It spun in the air and crashed once more onto the sea.

This time it did not submerge. It remained on the surface, rolling over and over, its tail lashing the water into a maelstrom of blood red foam.

Within seconds the pack, triggered now by the call of death, converged upon it. The sea boiled as huge, ravening mouths ripped the still-living body apart, tore ragged, bleeding chunks from the dying carcass.

A great scarlet stain began to spread out over the surface of the sea.

Andy averted his eyes. Nausea rose up in his gorge and he had to gulp it down, willing himself not to be sick.

He turned away.

Now, get away from here. Get away while they feed.

He threaded the sail rope through the pulley once more, tightened it, and let the sail fill. Then he sat down in the stern and began to draw away from the horror.

It had worked. The plan had worked. He was on his way again.

The joy, the relief were so intense he found himself to be almost crying. He shook with reaction for several minutes, but gradually the routine of sailing began to calm him.

Things were all right again. The danger was over.

Even the noises of the boat, which had so unsettled him, had made him so anxious when he first set out, now seemed comforting and familiar. The knock from the mast and the tap and thud of the steering oar felt like old, dependable friends helping him on his way.

He thought of his family back on *Quintana*.

It's all right, he called to them in his mind. *Don't worry. I'll see you soon.*

And so, convinced now of his success,

and proud that once more faced with a fearsome ordeal, he had survived it, he sailed on.

The shock of disappointment was therefore all the greater when, ten minutes later, the first of the sharks surfaced again a hundred yards off his port side.

He watched with horrified disbelief as the same pattern started all over again: the same mindless motion, the same implacable determination.

But this time it was too much. This time there were no possibilities of escape. This time there was only one outcome.

He was defeated. He had given all he had to give. He let the sail rope slip once more through his fingers, and the boat came to rest. The mast stopped banging against the block; the steering oar ceased its tapping.

Numbed now by the horror, he simply sat, anesthetized, drained of all emotion and all fear.

Resigned now to death, there was nothing to do but wait for it to take him.

It was over.

He stared out to sea, emotionless, as the sharks began to close.

Such are the strange forces that affect our lives and which, if we know of them, we call coincidence, that it was at that precise moment that Kaleku plunged his *larung* into the sea and called his sharks.

Come, shark, come, he heard it sing.

Come, shark, come.

The sound rippled out beneath him and echoed along the long undersea corridors of the shark roads, a sharp, penetrating clicking of wood on wood.

He shook it rhythmically in the way Sea-bird had taught him, pausing slightly between each shake to allow one sound to ripple away and be replaced, seconds later, by another, as though a voice called, siren-like, over and over.

Come, shark, come. Come, shark, come.

Two miles away the makos stopped, confused.

The sound they had followed had gone, faded into silence. But now here was a new one, calling them from far away.

This was an irresistible sound, a sound embedded in the dark recesses of their minds.

It was the clicking song of the great whales calling out over thousands of miles as they journeyed down to the icy southern oceans; it was the chatter of dolphins lolloping through surf; it was the rattle of the great shoals of tuna skittering through beds of waving seaweed; it was the cracking of bones as great fish fed on lesser, the thrashing of bird wings beating the surface of the sea, the death rattle of the injured turtle.

It spoke a simple message, the only message the shark wants or knows.

Eat!

The makos turned toward it, their prey forgotten. They circled briefly, locating the sound, then swung in from their places in the ordered pattern of the hunt and came together, twenty dark shapes in a tight, single-minded pack.

Then they submerged into the cool, dim depths of the shark road and accelerated away.

Perhaps at another time, or in another

place, Kaleku, the caller of sharks, would have stood a chance. But the world and the sea were in too much turmoil.

Perhaps if the sharks had not been maddened by the great rumblings and tearings of the earth, or swept to insanity by the sea's roaring turbulence, things might have been different.

Perhaps, even, if they had not still been gripped in the raging frenzy of the kill, he might have escaped.

But that was not to be.

Drawn along the urgent thread of sound, their minds filled with blood lust, the sharks roared into him from the west.

Kaleku hardly had time to know what was happening, no time at all to do anything, even if anything could have been done.

One moment he was sitting in the canoe, in a quiet, empty sea, shaking the *larung* and waiting patiently for a shark to appear.

The next, his canoe lurched right out of the water as the pack, hurtling vertically upward from the depths of the shark road, hammered into it and lifted it into the air.

Kaleku was hurled out.

He spun briefly, arms and legs flailing as uselessly as a rag doll's, and plunged, with a crash that winded him, into the sea.

Thrashing to the surface, he had time only to see the fins racing toward him.

He screamed once only before he died.

And, as he died, a single, vivid picture flashed across his brain.

A picture of a stone shark, ghost-gray under the moon, its carved mouth open, its white teeth luminous in the cold light.

And on its teeth, a scarlet stain of blood.

EPILOGUE

And so a young man's life was taken and another's given, though neither knew, nor ever would, of the existence of the other.

Old Sea-bird paddled into the shark road just before dark.

He had known where to go, and from the strange powers that had made him the greatest of the Shark Callers, had known before he had arrived what he would find.

Sadly he pulled the *larung* and *kasaman* out of the sea and cried a little for Kaleku, remembering the pride they had taken in the making of them.

Then he turned his back on the shattered remnants of the young man's life, pointed his canoe north, and paddled away.

———

Released from the terrible grip of the mako pack, Andy Thompson completed his journey.

Darkness, as he had guessed, had helped. Drawn by the lights of coastal village fires, he had eventually pulled into a small lagoon just after midnight. The village had been badly damaged by the tidal wave, but the villagers welcomed him and raised the alarm for him. The following morning a trawler left Kavieng, located *Quintana,* and towed her to safety. Three months later, repaired and proud again, she sailed out of Kavieng Harbor.

She is sailing still.

Old Sea-bird?

He never returned and now, of course, is long since dead.

But he is still there in the lonely shark roads of the oceans, calling his sharks. The men of New Ireland see him, from the corners of their eyes, at dusk, and just beyond their vision.

Sometimes, they say, there is another younger man with him.

GLOSSARY

brus tobacco

guria earthquake

kasaman propeller-shaped float for snaring sharks

lamat season of gentle southeast winds and calm seas

lap-lap length of cotton cloth worn by men wrapped around the waist, by women as a wrap-around dress

larangam sea-bird

larung rattle made from bamboo and coconut shells, for calling sharks

lavat season of strong northwest winds and rough seas

lembe shark

lesim dugout canoe

masalai spirits of the dead

motu big canoe

nuee ardente ("burning cloud") an incandescent cloud of gas, ash, and rock fragments, which flows rapidly over the ground after a volcanic eruption, destroying all life in its path.

pilai lizard

sing-sing songfest

tambu that which is forbidden

tsunami tidal wave

tulait the end of night and beginning of dawn

tumbuna an ancestor (*tumbuna* time—the ancestral past)

Mi go nau ("Me go now") I'm going

Orait All right

Yu go nau ("You go now") You're going